Mar... ...n ...

GUNTER
A Guide Dog

CasAnanda Publishing
Bayonet Point, Florida

GUNTER: *A Guide Dog*
by Marian Lund Modlin

Copyright 1996

Cover Photo: Jim O'Donnell

Request additional copies from your local bookstore or write:

GUNTER
Post Office Box 6253
Zephyrhills, Florida 33540

Printed in the United States of America
Library of Congress Cataloging-in-Publication Data
Marian Lund Modlin, date-
      Gunter: a guide dog: by Marian Lund Modlin
      p. cm.   Current PPD: 9611

CasAnanda Publishing
POB 7207
Bayonet Point, FL 34674
1-800-891-1064

Library of Congress Catalog Card Number 96-86794
ISBN: 1-889131-07-5 First Edition 1996
1. Human Interest   2. Self-Help

Dedicated to the memory
of those pioneers
of the guide dog movement
who discovered how humans and canines
can work together
in harmony and love.

CONTENTS

INTRODUCTION

Many persons who are blessed with normal vision are thrilled at the sight of a guide dog, confidently leading its blind master down the sidewalk. Their compassion for the visually impaired person is blended with their joy in watching how perfectly the trained guide dog carries out its task of guiding its master.

Today there are an estimated 16,000 guide dogs in the United States, teamed with visually impaired persons. The number increases by 5 to 7 per cent per year.

The concept of training dogs to lead the blind began in Germany at the close of the first World War. By the 1930's, Dorothy Eustis, an American widow living in Switzerland, was experimenting with skilled dog trainers to develop a working bond between dogs and blind people. Dorothy Eustis published an article about this in an American magazine, the Saturday Evening Post. It came to the attention of a young insurance salesman in Nashville, Tennessee, named Morris Frank. He had recently suffered the loss of his eyesight in a freak boxing accident. He believed that if he could obtain one of these trained guide dogs, it would enable him to resume his working career.

Morris Frank went to Switzerland and met Mrs. Eustis. He proved to be a good student. He completed the course of training with a female German Shepherd named Buddy, and returned to the United States with high hopes of going back to work selling insurance.

But at this time the American public was not ready to permit working dogs in business buildings, stores or restaurants. Taxicab drivers refused to carry a man with a dog, and dogs were not allowed on buses or trains. Morris Frank, as he returned to Nashville on the train, had to ride in the baggage car with his dog.

It was only after many years of diligent effort that state legislatures finally recognized the need and passed laws permitting blind persons to enter all public facilities with their guide dogs. Now every state protects this right. There are ten dog training schools in the United States where dogs are prepared for this specialized work.

The cost of training one person with a dog is estimated to run above $10,000. In most cases, these schools are supported entirely by voluntary contributions, receiving no tax money.

Many persons who have vision problems prefer to use a white cane, rather than learn to depend on a trained guide dog. Others have found that the dog restores their mobility, their ease of travel, without their constantly having to wait for someone else to take them where they want to go.

In most cases, the natural affection between a dog and its master becomes very strong. The two grow into a devoted, loving pair, bonded together for life.

In this frank and open account, Marian Lund Modlin tells of her experiences adjusting to life with a dog -- a person who was not a dog lover -- but a person who learned to love and to depend upon this special dog, Gunter, as her guide and her best friend.

GUNTER
A Guide Dog

Tires spun, horns honked, and engines raced. The city traffic was heavy. Gunter and I walked down the sidewalk beside the busy street. This was all new to me, and my heart thumped as we paced along. I puzzled over the sound of a motor as it grew louder. It didn't seem to be coming from the street. I was scared. Gunter slowed his pace.

"Forward, Gunter," I commanded.

Suddenly I felt Gunter as he shoved his body in front of me, stopping me from moving ahead. I felt the rush of wind as a van roared past. Gunter had just saved me from stepping in front of it.

As my heart settled back into place, I patted Gunter. "Good boy, Gunter. Good boy."

That was the first time I was aware of Gunter's training in "intelligent disobedience." And, that was the first time I realized the importance of my own training--learning to trust my dog. From that moment on, I knew that Gunter would protect me anywhere, from anything--even at the cost of his own life.

What I had just experienced was part of my own training, as well as Gunter's.

How does a puppy grow up to be a guide dog?

More importantly, how does the human-canine partnership develop the ability to function as a team?

Gunter's training for this work began when he was a strong, lively puppy in the home of Betty

Crowell of Palmetto, Florida. She still calls him her "grandson." His canine mother, Hope, is a sweet-tempered rough-coat Collie who looks a lot like Lassie. His father is a prize-winning smooth-coat Collie, champion of many shows.

To get ready for the arrival of the Collie babies, Betty had prepared a whelping place for the mother in a dry plastic children's' swimming pool in her home. At about 2:00 a.m. she heard a high-pitched yelp from this puppy, his first comment on arrival. He was the firstborn of the litter. She named him "Big Boy."

Betty gave much tenderness and love to the newborn puppies, together with friends Eva Divico and Barbara Anderson. By the time Big Boy was five weeks old, he was making regular visits to the nearby school of Southeastern Guide Dogs, Inc. There he met new people every day, wonderful people who love dogs and who volunteer their time to serve as "Puppyhuggers," playing with the cuddly puppies and teaching them to follow along as they are led on a leash. This helps the little ones to become socialized so they are openly friendly with each human they meet.

This plays an important part in the formation of the character of a guide dog. As Jan Sergeant of Southeastern Guide Dogs, Inc., explains it, "Because these dogs have been loved since day one, they love everybody. To them, every soul they meet is a potential friend."

After some twelve weeks of this, Big Boy went to live with a volunteer "Puppy Raiser," Stephanie Gunter, near Gainesville, Florida. She gave him her family name.

During his puppyhood Gunter was quite a barker, with a shrill, irritating voice. He barked often at lawn mowers and noisy trucks. Under Stephanie's loving care, he learned to control the impulse to bark. Southeastern's trainers often yell, "Quiet!" at the dogs in the kennels. As I think back to my own class, I don't believe we had a barker in the bunch.

Like all guide dog puppies, Gunter learned the social graces, not to beg for food at the table, and how to control his physical functions until taken to a relief area. Stephanie and her good friend Jill Clark, with Jill's sons Eric and Nathan, took Gunter on shopping trips to malls and shopping centers. He attracted much attention, wearing his blue and white blanket with the words "GUIDE DOG PUPPY."

With each human contact Gunter was developing a loving and caring attitude toward humans. He craved human attention and nothing pleased him more than to have someone walk up and chuck him under the chin or stroke the smooth white hair on his neck and shoulders. He still manages to keep his coat spotlessly clean. He is always licking his fur; sometimes I hear him doing it in the night. With the white blaze on his head, his fawn-colored back, his snow-white collar and paws, a little stripe of black hair going down toward the white tip at the end of his long tail, he looks so handsome that any dog lover would want to pet him.

By the time he was a year old, Gunter had grown into a regal-looking smooth-coat Collie, intelligent and alert, ready to learn the advanced skills of being a guide dog. He returned to the school at Palmetto for his lessons with professional trainers. Here he learned the forty commands necessary for a successful guide dog. He learned quickly.

Here, too, he found that his trainers and handlers were prone to mispronounce his name. Instead of sounding the "t," they made it "Gun-ther," like the name of a famous author of an earlier generation, John Gunther.

At the same time, my eyesight was failing due to macular degeneration. My husband, Harold, came upon a pamphlet describing Southeastern's training school for guide dogs at Palmetto, sixty miles from our home. The pamphlet listed the price of two dog harnesses at $250. We decided to visit the school and make a donation. At Palmetto, we delighted in the pleasant campus and met Director Mike Sergeant and his wife, Jan. She showed us a short movie about the school and about the training of a black Labrador guide dog named Yaz, with his visually impaired partner, Elisha Gilliland. Jan told us that Elisha had taken Yaz with her to law school at Vanderbilt University. In order to see the movie, I pulled my chair right up close to the screen. Jan asked me if I had a vision problem. I admitted that I did.

After the movie, Jan took us through the dormitory where the students stay while they are in school with their dogs; then we saw the kennels with about 75 dogs in training. Jan let us hold some of the tiny puppies who would grow up to be guide dogs.

We began to volunteer regularly at the school

as "dog walkers." About once a week, Harold drove us the sixty miles to the school, where we enjoyed leading the fully grown trainees out of the kennels for their exercise.

"How can I go about buying a guide dog?" I asked Mike.

"You can't," Mike said. "Nobody can buy one. The school will furnish a guide dog free to any person who needs it and is willing to undergo the necessary training with the dog."

The school receives no government funding. It is supported entirely by voluntary contributions. It is possible for a person to make a donation of the full cost of a dog. At that time the school was investing $8,600 in each dog it graduated. (It is higher now).

My husband and I were favorably impressed with the school and how it was operated.

As we drove home from our first visit, I remember that we talked about how the people we met, the trainers and dog handlers, all showed such a high regard for each individual dog. Instead of being lumped all together like a herd of cattle, the dogs were called by their own names and treated as individuals. Although the trainers were firm, they were also quite free with their love which they lavished upon the dogs. We could see that a little pause to scratch a dog's ear can go far to reassure the dog that he is loved.

As the weeks went by, we went often as volunteers to lead dogs at the school. We became acquainted with a number of friendly guide dogs-in-training, including a Labrador named Amy, an Australian Shepherd named Chester, a black

Goldador named Gordon. (Goldador is a Labrador-Golden Retriever cross); a Hungarian Vizsla named Fiddler; some German Shepherds, two smooth-coat Collie ladies named Leah and Lucy, and many more.

In fact, one of the Collies I remember leading several times was this big, friendly fellow we heard the trainers calling "Gunther." He seemed to walk with a serious purpose, yet without needlessly pulling forward too hard. He was never hurried or impatient, but always ready.

As volunteer dog walkers, we realized that we couldn't ask for any specific dog, but as we drove to the school for our regular visits, we were always hoping for a chance to see Gunter again. At this time he often was in Bradenton, with one of the trainers, learning how to go through court houses, on escalators, on buses and into stores. The trainers were getting him prepared, before he ever met his new master. Harold and I both began to adore Gunter and to look forward to taking him out for exercise.

To receive a guide dog, a visually impaired person must get an application form at the school. This calls for an eye doctor's signature and three personal references. This will take a while, then you will hear from the school. If you receive notice that you have been accepted, the school will give you a date several weeks ahead for the beginning of your class.

At first thought, I was not certain that I wanted to apply for a dog. I had not been what you would call a dog lover. I had grown up on an Iowa farm where the dogs lived outdoors. They were not like close members of the family. Then, too, I had misgivings about my own age.

"I'm 73, Mike," I confessed to the school director. "Isn't that too old to get a dog?"

"Marian, we had an eighty-four-year-old lady here. She had been a school teacher all her life. After her husband died, and she lost most of her eyesight to macular degeneration, she decided that she would get a guide dog. She's doing just fine."

That was when I decided, "If she can do it, I can too." I enrolled in the school, but I had to wait four months to get into a class. Finally, I was notified to join a new class starting in April. I need not have worried about age. My classmates ranged in age from 20 to 75.

The first day at school is spent listening to lectures and learning to handle the harness. On the second day the dogs are assigned to the students. I had been hoping that I would be lucky enough to get Gunter. Even though I was the smallest person in the class, and Gunter was the biggest dog, I felt that he had exactly the right personality to match mine. He had always been instantly responsive to my soft-spoken commands; I never had to yell at him or jerk him around by the collar when we walked together.

At last the trainer was ready to announce the assignment of dogs. I was tense with excitement. She began by saying that all of the dogs had been given a bath and groomed, ready to meet their new partners. As she brought the dogs in, one by one, I became more and more anxious. I sat there waiting to see which dog would be mine.

My dog was the sixth in line. The trainer

paused and said, "This is a fawn-and-white smooth-coat Collie male. Marian, what's his name?"

I was half laughing, half crying, as I shouted out, "It's Gunter!"

Then because she knew I couldn't see that far away, the trainer said, "Would you like to go to the other end of the room and meet him?"

With his tail wagging, he came bounding into my arms, kissing my face and letting me know he was happy to be my dog. I couldn't wait to get to a telephone to call my husband, but then I realized that I was not allowed to use the telephone until six o'clock.

Then another trainer, Rick, escorted me and Gunter to my room. I'm sure I chattered all the way to the room about how happy I was that Gunter was to be my partner. I felt very lucky that he had been chosen for me.

Rick said, "This is the beginning of your bonding process with your dog. Your first assignment is to take your dog into your room, and play with him for a half hour. Lie down on the floor beside him, talk to him, roll the ball with him."

This gave me the chance to talk to Gunter and tell him how great our life together was going to be. The half hour passed quickly because Gunter and I had a lot to talk about.

Promptly at six o'clock I took Gunter to the phone and we called my husband. Half crying, and with a lump in my throat, I told him that Gunter was the chosen one. He was happy to hear the news, for he had come to love Gunter too. This was the beginning of a wonderful partnership between human and canine, based on unfailing love, trust and respect for one another.

Now the big job lay ahead. The three of us would learn to live together in harmony.

There were fourteen persons in my class, nine totally blind and five, like me, with minimal eyesight. We were all ready for serious training.

In each dormitory room there were two dogs with their humans. Each twin bed had a dog tie-down attached to the nearby wall. During our second night together I was awakened by Gunter gently licking my bare foot. I realized then that this was an act of love, and that true bonding was beginning.

During our training period we students were never separated from our dogs. When we showered, the dogs went into the bathroom with us (each dormitory room had a bathroom). If we were called away to answer the phone, the dog went along.

Delicious meals were served, and at each meal the dogs stretched out on the floor under the tables while we ate. To simulate the conditions we would find in the outside world, the seats and tables were in a configuration just like those in various types of restaurants.

When Gunter and I were in training, Southeastern had twelve professional dog trainers. The number has since grown with the school. Part of Gunter's training consisted of learning how to walk in a straight line, how to go through revolving doors, how to board escalators and elevators, how to board buses without getting in someone's way, and how to avoid being distracted by cats that happen to stroll by.

As I became better acquainted with Gunter, I learned that he had received a tattoo mark in his left ear, coded in such a way that anyone at the school would know that this dog was the firstborn in his litter and a member of the "G" group born in 1992. We were enrolled together in the training class of April, 1994. I could see well enough to tell that he had a fine Collie head with brown velvet ears that perked up to catch every sound. One unique and endearing feature is his "blue merle" left eye. The other eye is a deep brown. Later, I learned that the blue merle gene shows up occasionally among Collies, Australian Shepherds, Huskies, and Alaskan Malamutes. It does not affect the dog's vision, but it gives him a distinctive appearance.

So now Gunter and I are a team, bonded together in love and respect for one another. Although I feel a deep sense of loss over my failing vision, I also feel a strong sense of pride as Gunter leads me down the sidewalk. This beautiful, highly trained creature helps me daily in many ways.

I was raised on a farm near Laurens, Iowa, in Pocahontas County. We had many large farm animals, plus the usual dogs and cats, but they all lived outside. None of our dogs ever got beyond the porch. We children were always told to wash our hands if we handled any of them.

Music was always an important part of my life. My parents both sang in the church choir and my father sang tenor in a male quartet for more than fifty years. He played many instruments. He bought me my first violin when I was four years old. I took lessons and studied it for ten years. After a year in college I applied for a position as a violinist with a choir based in Indianapolis. We traveled over most of the United States. I continued my violin studies at Arthur Jordan Conservatory of Music, connected with Butler University. I played in a symphony orchestra under the direction of Fabien Sevitzky.

At college I met my husband, Harold Modlin, who was studying radio. We married and had four children, Judy Hoefer, a nurse, Debby Snider, a high school and college English teacher, Dan Modlin, a radio newsman, and Belinda Arthur, who is trained as a licensed practical nurse and has recently entered the business of grooming dogs.

Our children and grandchildren have accepted Gunter as a member of the family. They call him their "little brother." Debby sent me a Mother's Day card on behalf of Gunter. It showed him asking, "Am I adopted?"

A friend says we should tell him, "No, you're not adopted. God sent you to us."

While our children were small, I stayed at home. When the youngest, Belinda, was four years old, I started substitute teaching, then I taught music in an elementary school for three years.

In the meantime my husband and I decided to start our own business. We called it Rural Radio Network. He was still working as an agricultural news and weather man for a TV and radio station in Indianapolis. I quit my teaching job and began a new career. Never having been in business before, I found it created a lot of pressure. We started in 1972 and the business grew quite rapidly. By 1975 we had five employees and were dealing with 57 radio stations. I made most of the decisions for the network, so I had a lot of responsibility, and I used my eyes constantly. I did not realize then that something was wrong with them.

In 1981 it was time for me to renew my driver's permit. When I got to the eye test, the license branch clerk said, "You're not reading those letters right." I said, "Oh, I know, I need my glasses changed."

She said, "You'd better see a doctor as soon as you can."

When I did, he discovered that I had lost the sight of one eye. I had not been aware of it. I was embarrassed.

"The brain compensates in a case like yours, Mrs. Modlin," the doctor told me. "Your problem is called macular degeneration."

I was familiar with the term because my mother and my aunt had it late in life. It was a bit scary, because I had no idea when it happened to me.

My sight gradually got worse, and by 1987, I lost my driver's permit. I immediately gave my car to my son. I didn't want it sitting there, where I could be reminded of my loss. My husband is a good driver and I've never been behind the wheel since.

For many years I had been an avid reader. When I retired, I was able to read large print with a very strong light. I had a commercial printer enlarge my violin music, so I began playing the violin again. I didn't want anybody to know that I had an eye problem. I tried to hide it.

But I still had many hobbies that required use of my eyes: needlepoint, oil painting, sewing, knitting. These were becoming almost impossible for me.

I began stumbling at curbs, and was constantly in fear of falling. I could see the forms of people moving about, but could not distinguish their faces. It got so I would panic when I couldn't see where my husband was.

Gradually as I shopped for groceries, I discovered that I could no longer read the marked prices.

I was becoming more discouraged because every eye doctor gave me the same answer, "There's nothing I can do for you."

At about this time Harold and I decided to visit Southeastern Guide Dogs, and we became volunteers. I wasn't sure that I could handle a dog and be fair to it. After talking with Mike and Jan at the school I signed up in November to take the training and get a dog of my own. My turn came the following April.

Getting a guide dog was not an easy decision. In many ways, it's like adopting a baby. There was a great deal of uncertainty involved. I didn't know that commands to use with the dog. I didn't know if I'd get a male or female. I didn't know if it would be a gentle, sweet tempered dog, or a tugging, pulling, fast-walking kind of a dog. I had really never been around anybody with a guide dog. I knew that this involved taking on a big responsibility. It's not like buying a sack of flour or a loaf of bread. It's a serious decision. You have to be prepared to be different from other people. You will lose your own identity to the dog. You will be known as "the blind lady," or "the person with a guide dog," or "the dog's mom."

But the advantages far outweigh the disadvantages. Just to look into Gunter's honest face and see his eagerness to help is a rewarding experience.

To enhance my remaining vision, I now have a closed circuit TV magnifier. It is a machine which greatly enlarges the printed page. I still love to cook and I can read my recipes on this big TV screen. Under the lens of the magnifier, I can see to write longhand on ruled paper. I use this for signing checks and other legal papers. In this way I can keep track of my personal business accounts. I also use it to magnify photographs of our great-grandchildren, which I could not see otherwise.

I enjoy my flowers; I have fifteen beautiful roses which Gunter and I feed and water. He always goes out with me; he loves to be outdoors.

I'm lucky to have a lady who comes in to clean my house every other week, and a yard man who comes when I need help with weeding my flowers and trimming the bushes.

The three of us, Harold, Gunter and I, go to church every Sunday. The dog is very good; we sit in a back seat and many of the people coming in say, "Good morning" to him. He shakes hands with them, as though he thoroughly enjoys greeting his friends. Gunter is included in our family picture in the church directory, with photo and name. He certainly has the best record for church attendance of any dog in our home town. During the services, he never tries to sing. I think that his active mind has made notations on each of his friends, and he recognizes them when he sees them come in.

Recently we attended a week of special Bible classes. At the end of the course, the director handed out diplomas to all who had attended. To my surprise, the director called Gunter up to the platform to receive his certificate, saying, "for good attendance, quiet manner, for never talking back, and always cooperating with the teacher."

I have continued to enjoy my music. Our string trio often plays in our own church and in retirement communities and nursing homes. Our friend Tom Warren, a concert violinist who is a veteran of many New York shows, joins me with my violin, and Harold with his guitar. Since I cannot see, I play now by memory. We play without amplification, striving for sweet tone and concentrating on the old familiar hymns and popular songs of the past. Stardust, Deep Purple, Tenderly, and Sweet Georgia Brown are among our favorites. Gunter is always a part of our concerts, shaking hands and greeting people who come by. I sometimes make a short talk explaining how the guide dog program works.

When we go out to eat, Gunter goes with us. All the restaurant people here know him and talk to him. He also goes with us to the local grocery store. One day, one of the employees, who used to have a dog obedience training business, came up and said, "I've noticed that your dog never sniffs the groceries."

I had noticed that, too, but I didn't tell her it's a different story when we come to the display of dog food bags. We hurry past them so Gunter won't be tempted.

Before Gunter came to our house, I was feeling very insecure. I worried about walking, because of my fear of stepping off curbs or stumbling over a crack in the sidewalk. I was afraid of falling over articles that had been left in the way. In short, I had lost my confidence.

It was really hard for me in talking to other people when I could no longer see their faces. I had taken "seeing" so much for granted. I never realized how much time and energy my eyes saved me, until I lost my vision. I have had to learn to be patient.

I was not aware that, for all my life, I had used my eyes to communicate. It was difficult for me to cope without seeing the reaction of the people I was talking with. I had not realized how much I depended on seeing the faces of others in a conversation.

I have learned that the eyes save you a lot of time and energy. It now takes me at least twice as long to do anything as when I had normal vision. I have had to learn to be patient. Day by day, Gunter has been a great help to me in making this adjustment.

Macular degeneration is a disease unfamiliar to many. The American Optometric Association says it is one of the primary causes of central vision loss in older Americans. Macular degeneration results from changes in the back of the eye which lead to blurring or loss of the center of your vision. As many as 25% of senior citizens are affected by this vision disorder. According to St. Luke's Cataract & Laser Institute of Tarpon Springs, Florida, total blindness seldom occurs in macular degeneration since peripheral vision is preserved even in the most severe cases.

Southeastern Guide Dogs notified me in November, 1993, that I would be enrolled in their class in April, 1994, and that I should walk two miles a day, to get in shape for working with a guide dog. I enjoy walking, so this was no problem. I was eager to get started, and it seemed to take forever for the days to pass while I waited.

We continued our once-a-week volunteering at the school, 60 miles from our home. This day the highlight of our week. There were several occasions when we invited friends to go with us. They were all interested in seeing the school and said afterward that they were glad they went. We would get up early enough to leave our house by 7:30 in the morning. This allowed time to make a breakfast stop at a fast food restaurant along the Interstate near Sun City Center. Usually it was a few minutes past 9:00 when we rolled up at the school, and there were already several cars parked near the kennels while volunteers stood in line to be handed a leash with the dog they would be leading that morning. There were from sixty to a hundred adult dogs needing to have their exercise. The school trains several different breeds, and this gave me a chance to get acquainted with the personalities of the various kinds of dogs. I soon began to love them all. We would also see puppy huggers sitting in comfortable chairs holding these cute little balls of fur, teaching them to get used to the human touch. Sometimes the puppy huggers take the little ones out for practice at being led on a leash. Everyone seemed to be having a great time. We used to laugh about how this was just like going out to play golf, because the grounds were so beautiful, only instead of hitting a golf ball around, we were exercising the dogs-in-training.

The volunteers usually lead the bigger dogs down a dead-end country road among the orange groves; there is seldom much traffic to interfere. It's amusing to see how excited the dogs get, running from bush to bush, pulling at the leash in their exuberance at being out in the open country. These dogs are not wearing their guide dog harnesses, so they are free to be like any other dog. Each dog has spent a lifetime in training, in order to become a good guide dog.

Volunteers do not do any training; all we did was provide exercise and socialization. The dogs dearly love this. On different days we were given different dogs to lead. Each one was lovable in its own way and we enjoyed seeing how each dog reacted to human attention. As a group of people walked down the road with their dogs, it was interesting to notice how happy everyone was: both dogs and people.

Dog walking usually ends with the volunteers grooming the dogs. The school provides combs and brushes. I was surprised to see how much pleasure grooming gives a dog.

During the months of waiting, I was a little apprehensive about getting a guide dog. It was to be a new experience for me, something different. There is only one other guide dog in our home town. I worried about how we would be accepted among our friends in church if we came in with a guide dog. We eat out often, and I was concerned about taking a dog into a restaurant. I knew that we had a legal right to take a guide dog anywhere, but I wondered how these people would really feel about it. We talked to managers of several eating places to get their reactions.

One of the ladies said, "Oh, I'm so glad you're getting a dog. My mother's eyesight is failing and I had always wanted her to get a dog, but it never worked out."

A restaurant owner said, "My father's eyesight has really failed him. Several years ago I had hoped that he would get a dog, because I think the guide dog system is wonderful." Everyone I talked with assured me that the dog would always be welcome in their places of business.

One reason I was hesitant is that I had always tried to hide my eye condition. I didn't want people to know of my problem. If you walk down the street holding to your husband's arm nobody thinks anything about it. But if you walk down the street holding a guide dog's harness in your hand, you are not merely saying, "I have an eye problem." You are telling the world, "I can't see."

My friends with eye problems seem to feel the same way. When I mention a dog to them, or suggest that they apply for talking books, or get magnifying lenses, a video reading machine, or anything of that nature, the first thing they say is, "I'm not ready for that." I always quote Jim O'Donnell, one of my instructors at Southeastern:

"You're getting your dog at the perfect time, Marian," he said. "Most people wait ten years too long. It's much easier to adjust while you still have a little sight."

Finally, the days of waiting passed, and it was time for me to leave for my training. Clothing for all sorts of weather conditions had to be considered for my 26-day stay on the campus. April in Florida can bring lots of surprises, from rain, to hot, to cool weather. Along with personal necessities, I was told to bring a battery-operated cassette tape recorder, with a large supply of blank cassettes. I knew this meant there would be many lectures which I would want to record on tape.

Additionally, to help me pass the time between classes, I brought along my cassette recorder which is furnished by the Talking Books organization, and a large supply of these "books" to listen to.

My violin has always been a part of my life, so I brought it with me to the school. Secretly, I worried that my dog would howl at the sound of violin music, as some dogs do. I wanted to introduce him to the instrument early, to be sure that the dog would be comfortable with its sound.

Before my classes began, we corresponded several times with the school. We offered to put up a fence to enclose the lawn, or to string up a long wire in the yard between posts, where the dog would be free to run. We also offered to enclose a screened-in porch. We found that the school prefers what is called "leash relief" for the dog, rather than turning it loose in an enclosure. You take the dog out on a leash and give it the command,

"Busy, busy."

When my husband took me to the school, it took a long time to unload and carry in all the things I had brought for my 26 days away from home.

I was shown to my well-furnished room and noticed that it had a nice walk-in closet and a bathroom for the two students who would share the room. At the end of each bed there was a tie-down for a dog. The dormitory had a women's wing and a men's wing. All the rooms had attractive home made quilts on the beds. The quilts had been donated by a puppy raiser who made them.

At this point, I met my new room mate, Ann Vick, a nice lady from Arkansas, about my age, who had about the same amount of vision that I had. She was there to train with a new dog, after her previous dog had been retired.

I reluctantly said goodbye to my husband. When I heard him driving away, I realized that he could not come to visit me except for four hours on Saturdays and four hours on Sundays. This was going to be an adjustment for the two of us. During our marriage, we had not had many times of separation except when he was away on business travel. At this time he had just returned from a farm reporting trip to Japan. I was beginning to see that such separations would be much easier for me if I had a guide dog at home with me.

When I met the other members of my class, I found that the ages ranged from 20 to 75. As was to be expected, there was a wide variety of occupations. My room mate had been a secretary at a law school. One student was a bilingual insurance man from

Miami; he was translating for another man who understood only Spanish.

There was a minister in the class, a man who had some eyesight. He came to the school, bent over and tapping along the hallways with a white cane. Ann and I told him his wife would be proud to see how handsome he would look, walking upright with his black Labrador dog instead of the cane. He had come to the school thinking he would need both the cane and the dog, but this encouraged him to understand that he could get along now without the cane.

There was a man whose eyes had been injured in the service. His previous guide dog had been a German Shepherd and this time the school gave him a black Labrador, a much smaller dog than he was used to. After a few days I noticed that the school had switched dogs for him and had given him a German Shepherd. He was very happy with it.

There was a horse rancher from Texas who had been blinded in a gun accident. He got a cute little Australian Shepherd. He told me that his plans were to take the dog on the horse with him as he rode on the ranch; then at his destination they would dismount and the dog could lead him to wherever he wanted to walk. Since I had been raised on a farm, I could see how the dog might be very happy riding with his master on the horse and leading his human partner around the ranch. Another young man had just lost a second eye about thirty days before he came to the class. He was in a state of mourning his loss. All of us felt very close to him. He was my training partner several times as we walked with our dogs in Tampa, and it seemed to me that he got along very well.

There were two younger girls, each training for a second dog. One was completely blind. She was my partner on a shopping trip to the mall where we looked for a gift for her boyfriend. The clerk was very helpful.

There was a young man from Texas who managed a concession stand on the beach. He got a German Shepherd.

A man from Alabama was in school to get a replacement dog. He worked for the library department of services for the blind in his state. Some evenings several of us played cards in the dining room. While we played, our dogs lay under the table. We used a card deck marked with large numbers and with Braille markings. I was amazed to find that this man could keep score in his mind; he could tell each of us what our score was at any time.

Another girl worked in vocational training for the handicapped. She got a little black Labrador.

We all came to be good friends as we completed our course of study. We had come from many different backgrounds, bringing with us many different needs, but through the discipline of the school we had been made members of a fantastic partnership: humans and canines working together.

In comparing the dogs, I discovered that Gunter was the largest dog in my class, while I was the smallest person. I was so happy that the trainers had decided to give me this big, beautiful sable and white smooth-coat Collie. Obviously they felt that his easy-going pace and gentle disposition were perfect for me. How could I have been so lucky?

When we settled into our daily routine, the dogs were with us twenty-four hours a day, to establish the bonding process. My room mate also got a smooth-coat Collie. He was a beautiful pepper-and-salt spotted male named U.B. He was a half-brother of Gunter, about the same size, and they got along perfectly with one another.

Our days began with a knock on the door at 6:00 a.m.; you had time to shower. You take your dog right into the bathroom for this, then you dress and take the dog out for relief on the grassy area outside the dorm. Then it's time for breakfast at 7:00. It's a hearty meal, to get you ready for the day. Instead of just boxed cereals, the cook served a great variety of foods and usually a glass of freshly squeezed orange juice. What could be more tasty than orange juice sipped within sight of the rich green citrus groves of central Florida? Snacks were available throughout the day, and there was always a bowl of fruit. Many times the cook made cookies and you could go to the kitchen to get them.

Immediately after breakfast, we spent a half hour working on "obedience." Dogs have to learn, with their masters, to concentrate, and not to be distracted by passing cats or golf carts. The dogs learn to watch their masters intently so as not to miss a signal. To begin, you use the long leash and tell your dog to "Stay," as you back away.

Students are told that they should review "Obedience" with the dog twice each day. This consists of "Sit," "Down," "Heel," "Stay," and "Come."

For the obedience drill, each person got in line with his or her dog. The instructor would go up or down the line and tell us individually what command to give our dog. Usually the dogs were not all performing at the same time.

To test the dog's ability to concentrate, sometimes the instructor would unexpectedly throw a ball, and the dog was not supposed to move. She would also bring cats to the training session and the dogs were supposed to ignore them.

The first day at school we were introduced to the harness. It is made to fit the dog's body with a strap behind the front legs. The handle extends up toward the person's hand, and you also hold the end of his leash, which is connected to a neck chain. Gunter's harness has a large red and white sign saying, "DO NOT PET ME. I AM A WORKING SOUTHEASTERN GUIDE DOG." For right-handed people, the dog is trained to walk on the person's left, always choosing a path that will allow room for the person walking beside him. I understand that a dog can be trained the other way, to walk on the right side, beside a left-handed person.

Gunter is very good about giving me plenty of room in a tight situation and I have never bumped into anything. We were warned always to hang the harness in a closet when it is not in use, because some dogs like to chew on the leather, and they might damage it. During my training time, I left Gunter's harness lying on the bed in my dormitory room with the door open. Mike happened to walk by and see it. He immediately told me to hang the harness in the closet. I never forgot again. In fact, one member of my class made that mistake, and his dog destroyed the leash, which he had to replace.

Certain days of the week, we would go into the school's campus in Bradenton, taking two of the school vans. It was difficult for me to learn the correct way to board the van with my dog: I was supposed to make the lead long and command Gunter to "Stay." Climb aboard and move toward a seat saying, "Gunter, come." Then sit down and find a place for him near me.

Sometimes the trainers became very impatient with me because they thought I didn't yell loud enough at my dog, or jerk it around by the choke chain the way some people do with their dogs. I always felt that this dog did not require jerking around or shouting.

I said, "I didn't yell at my four children; why should I start yelling at my dog?" I realize that it takes a lot of firm discipline to teach a dog all these wonderful things in five or six months' time. Throughout our training, Gunter was a gentle giant, instantly responsive to my soft-spoken commands.

The school's Bradenton branch gives the students a place to practice walking in city traffic. Most of the time we worked in pairs under the supervision of a professional trainer. The dog had already learned to stop at all curbs and obstacles, alleys and intersections. Humans had to remember all strange obstacles such as bumps in the sidewalk, to help us keep track of where we were.

At traffic lights we learned to wait, listening through two or three light changes to get the rhythm of the traffic flow before giving the dog the "forward" command.

We rode city buses to shopping malls. To board a bus with the dog requires a different skill from what we learned on the school vans. To board a city bus, Gunter goes first into the bus, ahead of me, and waits while I pay the fare. Then I give him the command, "Gunter, find an empty seat." Immediately, he leads me to a vacant seat, because he has been taught to move quickly and get out of peoples' way.

At a pet store Gunter enjoyed sniffing the dog food bags. He was intrigued by the live parrots in the display window. He watched them with intense interest. I let him take a little time to enjoy this. It was almost as if I could hear him saying, "Momma, buy me one of those to take home." He watches the kittens and puppies in a pet store, but for some reason it's the birds that have the strongest attraction to him. He only watches them; he never tries to give chase.

We went to a large city parking lot. Our dogs led us down a narrow pathway between lamp posts and parking meters. At the end of this walk, our instructor said, "Marian, do you realize that Gunter took you around more than two hundred parking meters and you never touched a one?"

At noon, various volunteer groups would bring our lunch. We would all sit in a square, facing each other and talking over the events of the morning. Our dogs would lie under the table while we ate.

Certain days we rode to Tampa for practice walking in big city traffic. We also learned to avoid obstacles and the large crowds of people on the sidewalks, especially at the noon hour. Many times people would step aside when they saw us coming. Gunter would always lead me around manholes, scaffolds, or any unusual object. At no time did Gunter ever let me bump into anyone or anything. He knows he is in charge, and responsible for my safety.

We learned how to go with our dogs through revolving doors and how to get on elevators. Gunter always points his nose right at the call button for an elevator. I can feel with my right hand just where his nose is pointing, and find the button. Then when the doors open he walks politely to the back of the elevator to keep us out of the way of the other people. He cannot tell me which floor the elevator is on. Sometimes I can count the buttons and punch the right floor; other times I have to ask other people what floor the elevator is on.

In leaving a hotel room, it's often helpful to mark the door knob with a ribbon or rubber band, so it feels different from the other knobs; this helps you find it when you come back to the room. Sometimes the dog can take you directly to your room, guided only by the scent. Gunter loves escalators; as soon as he sees one ahead, his tail begins to wag with excitement as he leads me to it.

My partner and I, with our dogs and our instructor, walked through a park where there was a fountain with a pool of water. The instructor warned my partner to hold his Labrador back because it might want to pull away and get into the water. I had no trouble with Gunter. He doesn't like to get his feet wet.

In this park we practiced going up and down steps, then the dog trainer took us to a rather exclusive dining room for a Dutch treat lunch. We ate comfortably while our dogs rested under the table.

Our instructor said, "We probably should make a bathroom stop here, but the restrooms are down stairs and they'd be very crowded. All three agreed to wait until we found another one. We walked to a fast food restaurant nearby and when I got into the restroom, I had a hard time getting my big dog into the stall. When it was time to leave, I realized that the door swung toward the inside and I didn't see how we were going to get out! I mentally debated whether I should yell for help. My weight was only 110 pounds, and my dog 85. If I had been a heavyweight myself, it would have been a serious problem. As it was, Gunter and I finally squeezed out on our own. Ever since then, I look for a handicapped stall which allows plenty of room for Gunter, or else I'll ask my husband to wait outside with the dog.

On the second Sunday of our training, my roommate's husband flew in from Arkansas and rented a compact car to take us to worship in a church about a half mile down the road from the school. I sat in the back seat of this little car with two big 85-pound guide dogs. Ann's husband got out and went to the door of the church. He came back with a man who held out his arm and said, "I am your escort."

As we entered the church, I said a little prayer

that we would be able to find seats in the back of the crowded sanctuary. I was nervous because I had never taken a dog to church before. It's kind of like taking a baby to church for the first time. You wonder how the dog will react. Inside, we found that there was a back seat available and we all sat down in it.

When the minister got up, he said, "We have guests with us this morning from our well respected neighbor, Southeastern Guide Dog School. We all know that working dogs should not be touched and I hope that you will respect their wishes and make them welcome."

Both dogs behaved like perfect gentlemen. Afterward, Ann and I laughed to think that we were being treated like royalty because of Gunter and U.B.

On one of Harold's week-end visits, he brought a tennis ball and Gunter enjoyed a brisk game of pitch and catch. Gunter can devote his attention completely to his work, but when his harness is off, he is always ready for play time.

The first week-end that we were permitted to leave the campus, Harold and I decided to go out to eat in a restaurant, taking Gunter with us. As we approached our car, Harold opened the door to the back seat and I said, "Gunter, get in the car." He just stood there looking at me. It was then I realized that he was used to riding in a van. A car was unfamiliar to him. It ended up with the two humans lifting this 85-pound dog into the car. After we came home with Gunter, we gave him several lessons on different ways to get into and out of a car. He learned quickly, and soon he was doing it with ease and charm. Now it's a joy to watch him as he steps out of a car, his front feet down on the pavement first, his rear parts seeming to float down in a step as graceful as that of a ballet dancer. The fact is that in his previous homes, Gunter had always been with people who drove vans, so he had no need to learn about boarding an automobile.

I'm told that Southeastern now includes instruction in boarding cars and taxis.

For every class of students at Southeastern, there is one highlight called "Puppy Raisers Day." The families who have taken these growing puppies into their homes and sent them off to school are invited to come in to meet the person that the dog will be guiding, and watch the new partners in action.

This was a big day for Gunter, and for me. He saw his grandma and his baby sitter, and my husband. By now Gunter considered Harold one of his best friends. It was a very nervous day for me, because being responsible for a dog was still a new experience. Gunter became very excited and jumped around and wagged his tail a lot. Flashbulbs were going off everywhere. Gunter's babysitter, Jill, brought him a bag of toys and handed me a photo album that showed his growth and development from puppyhood up to his entrance into advanced training.

"Puppy Raisers' Day" had been memorable, but school wasn't over yet.

One outstanding trip I remember from school was when we all took our dogs to the grocery store for the first time. The trainer told me, "Take Gunter up and down the aisle by yourself." Naturally I was uneasy, but after the first aisle, I was surprised to see that this dog actually knew "left" and "right" in a working situation. There are three ways of telling the dog "left" and "right." One is to wave the direction with your right hand over his face so he can see where you want to go. The second is to use the leash by pulling it to the right or left. The third is by the vocal command. This is the one I use mostly; I just say, "Gunter, left;" or "Gunter, right," and I seldom have to repeat the command.

In this big store, we went up and down all the aisles, and I was thrilled from my toes on up, to know that this dog would respond so perfectly to my spoken commands.

During each day's activities, we had to be back at the school by four o'clock, in time for the dogs' feeding. One of the trainers cautioned me always to make sure Gunter had ample time to drink his water, because a Collie's tongue is only half as wide as another dog's; therefore he doesn't get as much water in each lap.

Sometimes we took night walks in the city for practice, and one day we had a country road walk in which Gunter learned to find the mail box on command. Gunter also showed me that he had been taught to take me three steps off the road if a car came along, for our safety. He has never forgotten this procedure.

One afternoon we had a class on bathing and grooming our dogs. In Florida this can be done outside with a garden hose most of the year.

This is not one of Gunter's favorite activities,

for he doesn't like to get in the water. He is not a water dog. He acts as though he thinks, "Marian wants me to do this, so I'll put up with it but I don't have to enjoy it." I have found that a bathing suit is my best garment for his bath. Sometimes I give him his bath indoors in the walk-in shower.

On our final day at school, Mike called me in and told me that Gunter and I had graduated. "Gunter is now your dog. Take him home," he said. "Enjoy working with him. Remember that your dog loves you. He wants to please you by meeting your every need. You are in control of whether or not this will be a good team, but both the master and the dog have to put their hearts into this work together."

Harold came to the school to get me. We loaded all of Gunter's belongings and mine into the car and invited Gunter to climb into the back seat. The three of us, as a family, started for home.

"Give Gunter all the time he wants to sniff out his new home," Mike advised. The place will be strange to him, and he needs time to inspect his new surroundings."

We two humans went from room to room with Gunter as he explored the house. He really seemed to enjoy looking around, and it appeared that he knew this was going to be his new home.

Months before, when I decided to go ahead and train with a dog, I had asked the school what improvements we might make in our home, such as a glassed-in porch, a fenced-in yard, or a long wire between posts to give the dog a running area. I learned that the school favors "leash relief," taking the dog out each time for its physical functions. No fence or enclosure is necessary. We added a sliding screen door to our garage. Gunter enjoys lying in the garage on a mild day and looking out through the screen door, savoring all the scents that come drifting by. This also enables him to see what's going on in the neighborhood.

He had no trouble adjusting to the relief area we had chosen for him. Behind our house, where I led him on the leash, he responded readily to my command, "Busy, busy."

One reason I chose to apply for a dog was my desire to live an active life. I had undergone a period of grieving when my eyesight failed, and I had to restrict my activities. I longed for those happy days when I drove my own car and traveled about the state attending business meetings and recording radio interviews for our farm broadcasting network. The guide dog could not replace my driver's license, but he could make it possible for me to travel on public transportation.

My husband and I had moved toward our retirement years sharing a fondness for travel. We visited Switzerland ten times in ten successive years, and toured with various farm groups in Europe, Australia, New Zealand and South America. We had been very active.

Now, with the dog, it is possible to travel again. We have made several air trips with Gunter on domestic airlines and had no difficulties. Usually we request seats directly behind the bulkhead. The airline personnel go out of their way to allow Gunter plenty of floor space in the aircraft. During take-off, when human passengers are nervously tapping their fingers on the arm rest or chewing gum, Gunter is calmly resting on the floor in front of us. As long as he can be close to me, he feels that this is his post of duty, and he is very calm about it.

The airlines never require a ticket for a guide dog. The other passengers are always friendly and helpful, offering compliments on his good looks and gentle behavior. More about air travel with a guide dog in Chapter 7.

I think I can say that Gunter has greatly enhanced our enjoyment of travel by giving me the gift of mobility.

Since he has become a part of our family, we have taken several long automobile trips. He never seems reluctant to get in the car. He hops out when we call him to visit a rest area, and, if we choose to go to a restaurant, he is always ready to lead us. People along the way are nice to us. They frequently ask questions that reveal their interest.

I have asked my husband to give his account of the adventure of bringing a guide dog into our home.

Harold: When Marian first talked to me about a guide dog, I guess I didn't actually realize how bad her eyesight had become. For some reason, I kept putting off the visit she had asked to make to the dog school. Then finally the day came. As I drove the unfamiliar territory around Palmetto, I got lost looking for the Southeastern campus. I drove into the city of Palmetto, which is not the right way to get to the school from our house. Totally lost, I stopped the car and dialed the number of the school. I told the person on the phone where I was and she gave me explicit instructions on how to find the school: "On Interstate 75, take Exit # 45 and go west on Moccasin Wallow Road to the first flasher light; turn left and go about one mile; cross the bridge, and you'll see the school on your left." With those instructions, I found it.

I know that I really did want her to get a dog. More and more I had come to realize how little she could see. She truly needed a guide dog.

The thought of bringing a dog into our home did not bother me. We had raised four children, but now they were all grown up and on their own, living in their own homes. In retirement, we were living in a comfortable new home in Florida, fully enjoying our later years together.

I had grown up with the benefit of the constant companionship of a loving dog, Buster. He was the loyal friend of my boyhood, for I had no living brothers or sisters. A boy growing up on a farm in the 1920's and '30's would have had a lonely life without a dog.

With happy childhood memories of woodland rambles with Buster, I began to look forward to welcoming a guide dog as a part of our family.

During our marriage, Marian and I had not experienced long periods of separation, so the 26 days of her time on the Southeastern Campus passed very slowly for me. During the first weeks, the students and dogs were not permitted to leave the campus. This was to help the bonding process. On the night when she phoned me to give me the good news that Gunter was to be her dog, I rejoiced with her. I was already acquainted with this beautiful smooth-coat Collie, remembering him from the days that Marian and I had spent volunteering as dog walkers at the school.

I loved Gunter for his willing spirit, his loyalty, his friendliness, his sense of devotion to duty. On every weekend when visits were permitted, I hurried down to the school to spend all the time I could with these two loved ones of mine.

I never had any doubts that Gunter was the right dog for Marian. As we became better acquainted, through my visits on week-ends at the school, I could see that Gunter was accepting me. He loved Marian, so therefore he loved me.

I think that Marian was helping this along,

giving Gunter a hint when she was expecting me for a visit. The two of them would be waiting on the screened-in porch at the dormitory, Gunter lying under her chair. Marian could tell by Gunter's actions when I drove in and parked. The moment he saw me approaching, he would get up and watch intently while I got out of the car and walked closer. I could see his ears pointing straight up as he looked intently in my direction. Then he would get all excited in anticipation, and lead her over to meet me. When I came closer and stroked his head, he would go wild with joy as he welcomed me. It was not hard for me to learn to love this adoring creature.

During my visits, we simply walked together about the shady campus or sat and talked on one of the big red and white benches, with Gunter at our side.

One thing I quickly noticed about Gunter and Marian, compared to the other students: Marian's voice was always soft and gentle as she spoke to him. And he would stand listening to her, enraptured. After watching him, I believe that Gunter thinks her voice is the sweetest music his ears had ever heard.

Now in his third year with Marian, this lucky dog still hears Marian's soft-spoken commands and responds in perfect love. She doesn't sound like someone talking to a dog; she sounds like a gentle person talking to someone she loves.

As Marian's husband, I have often been tempted to think of Gunter as "my" dog, to take over and control his feeding and snacking. But I must not do this. I realize that, while I love him, I must respect Marian's and Gunter's devotion to one another. I thoroughly enjoy my friendship with him. I get a lot of pleasure out of taking him on long walks. We leave his guide dog harness at home and he goes beside me on a long leash. This is something the two of us share--a companionship, not of "master and dog," but of two living beings enjoying one another's company, observing together the sights and sounds of the day. And I think, surely the Creator knew what He was doing when He planned for dogs to be the loving helpers and friends of mankind.

Now that I am older, my thoughts go back to my boyhood and the love I shared with my little black and tan dog, Buster. As we walk along, I see Gunter occasionally glancing up at my face, as if to say, "Am I doing all right?" I reassure him with a gentle pat on the head and he goes on happily.

As we walk together, I frequently say things to Gunter, always in a soft, gentle voice, like telling him what a good dog he is. I remember that his name, when he was a newborn puppy, was "Big Boy." This is what I call him.

It doesn't hurt my relationship with Gunter for me to realize that I am not the "top dog" at our house. I'm just happy to be a good friend of the top dog.

Gunter has given me the travel mobility that I wanted after my eyesight failed. He is a perfect traveling partner and is always willing to go when we are ready.

Still, he can be a great homebody, an ideal companion for an elderly lady and her husband when they choose not to travel.

When he is leading me, he gives total concentration to the task. Then, when his harness is removed at home, he is ready to relax completely. He will stretch out on the floor and sleep for an hour or two, replenishing his energy.

When a family takes a dog into their home, it is obvious that some adjustments must be made. One of our friends said to Harold, "Well, you're not going to be top dog at your house any more."

I'm glad for the fact that my husband is a dog lover. He welcomed Gunter with joy. And it's evident that Gunter knows how to be "Dad's Boy." When Harold sits down in an easy chair to read, Gunter often walks over to the chair and extends a paw for a handshake. Most guide dogs do not shake hands, but Gunter learned this in his earliest puppyhood training. Betty Crowell taught him to "give paw," based on the old German dog command, "Gibt Pfoechen." And this dog never forgets.

He still remembers how, as a little puppy, he used to be able to sit in the laps of his human friends. Now that he is an 85-pound giant, he still wants to do it. He struggles to back up onto a sitting person's lap, as if he thinks it is still possible for him to be held on a human's lap. He pants, and his tongue hangs out as he leans against your legs; he maneuvers and pushes his body as far as he can against you. He puts his two hind legs on the chair as he endeavors to climb up. He often does this when he sees that we are sitting in a chair putting on stockings. He is never mean about it; this is simply his way of showing us that he loves us. Our friends tell us they've never seen a dog do this before.

At first we were careful to keep him off the beds and sofas in our house. Later, as we came to accept him more fully as a member of our household, we decided that he should feel welcome anywhere in the house. Now I always spread clean cotton sheets over the beds and the davenport. It's so easy to wash sheets. Our dog-trainers may not approve of this leniency, but Gunter is such a well behaved personality that we allow him to hop up on the bed with us. He does this with grace. His warm body is a source of much comfort as he snuggles up against his human friends.

When he first came to live with us, Gunter had not learned how to get on a bed. It only took a few lessons and he got the knack of running and leaping up with elegant dignity.

Gunter formed the habit of rising in the early morning when we were in training together at the guide dog school. Now that we are all at home, he counts on Harold to be available for the early feeding and walk. Being a farm broadcaster, Harold has been an early riser all of our married life. He also is a diabetic who needs daily morning exercise. Gunter awakens Harold with a soft nudge of the nose; if he gets no response, he uses his voice to alert his partner. He doesn't bark; he just speaks one soft word, "Out."

Yes, you may doubt this if you will, but this dog clearly enunciates the word "out" when he feels the need to go out. (He may be a little weak on the final sound of the "t," but there is no mistaking his vocal request).

On their morning walks, of course, Gunter is on a long leash, not in his guide dog harness. This way he can enjoy just being a dog, stopping to sniff the bushes and posts along the way. I don't think it damages my bond with Gunter if my husband answers his morning wake-up call.

Besides, what human could resist the plaintive voice of a loving dog saying, "Out?"

After their morning walk, Gunter expects to play a game of Frisbee with a soft lambskin disk, which Harold throws in the back yard. Gunter races to retrieve it with a great burst of energy, and brings it back happily with a big wag of his white-tipped tail. When Harold says the game is over, Gunter picks up the Frisbee and carries it into the house. Then, my husband admits, they both go back to bed for a morning nap.

Later in the day, I put Gunter's harness on him and we go for a walk in our neighborhood. I tell him to take me to the mail box, and he leads me down the sidewalk to the correct drive. We have sidewalks and well-lighted streets, so we can walk day or night. We often come upon flocks of friendly ducks, and occasionally a squirrel will run up a tree nearby. Cats in the neighborhood ignore Gunter and he gives them the same treatment. Gunter always sees every movement, but he is never tempted to give chase. He is self-disciplined. As we walk, if he hears a car start up in a garage two or three houses ahead of us, he will let me know. He goes into a prancing walk. I can detect instantly by his actions that somebody is around, doing something different. As I walk in the neighborhood, I often stop to visit with friends. Gunter always waits patiently for me as long as I stand talking. He never tries to hurry on. Many of our neighbors have lawn sprinkling systems. When Gunter sees the fine spray, he stops cold. He doesn't look at me, but he throws his head toward me enough that I know I had better not go on. I trust his judgment, because sometimes the water is such a fine little spray that I can't see it; but he can. He avoids taking me onto a water-soaked sidewalk by leading me out into the edge of the street so we won't get wet. He definitely wants to keep his paws dry. He doesn't want me to get wet either. It's the same way after a rain, when there are puddles remaining. When he stops, I always pay attention to him. Unlike many guide dogs, Gunter is always reluctant to go out in the rain. However, he never shows any fear of storms, even when there is lightning and thunder.

We have never had a flea problem with this dog. We have our house and lawn treated once every two months by a professional pest control firm. When I give him a bath, I use a flea-control shampoo. When I groom him, I can't see fleas myself, but my husband checks the combings carefully. I use Skin-So-Soft on him regularly, rubbing it on his hair sparingly with a damp cloth. It's the only bug repellent that he likes. The others offend his sense of smell. The minute I get an aerosol bottle off the shelf, he runs; he doesn't like any of this stuff. If I get any of it on him, he runs to the living room and rolls on the carpet, trying to get rid of that smell, and making funny noises in his throat like he was trying to cough it up. He looks at me reproachfully, as though to say, "You know I don't like that stuff." Inside the house, we still have a tie-down for him, but it is seldom used. Gunter has the run of the house. The trainers at the school recommended that the first thirty days we keep him on the tie-down, especially at night, and most of the day. When he first came to live with us we discovered that he liked the cool, smooth surface of a tile floor for his nap in warm weather. He avoided the rug. So we had a patch of carpeting in the hall taken up and had it replaced with tile, just to make a comfortable place for him to lie. He tells us he likes it; he uses it often.

On those occasions when we return from a trip, it's delightful to see how happy Gunter is to be home again. Before arriving at our house, we talk to him about going home. We are quite sure he understands. When he gets out of the car at home, he walks all around, sniffing the familiar scents of our yard. He goes into the house with great excitement, running around the dining table, enjoying every moment of being at home again.

When we sit down to eat, he always lies on the

floor at our feet, never begging for food, never even sniffing to identify what we are eating.

Some dogs have been known to snitch food from the table. Gunter never does this. He knows where we keep a bowl of his treats. He often stands by the bowl, a hopeful look on his face, but he never tries to jump up and grab one.

I have always been a flower lover, and even though my eyesight is dim, I still enjoy working with my roses, petunias, camellias and hibiscus. When I garden, Gunter always goes outdoors with me to lie in the soft grass nearby.

Gunter has a very sensitive nose. When my husband brings the mail into the house, Gunter usually lies beside the table while he opens the letters. If there is something from our friends who have dogs, he gets up and wags his tail with excitement, as though he expected to receive a message. Harold lets him get the scent of the mail. He gets all excited and as Harold holds the letter for him to sniff, his nose goes back and forth over it. To see him, you would think that he is reading the letter, line by line with his nose.

When I am at the mall and people stop me to ask questions about the dog, he sniffs their shoes. I ask them, "Do you have a dog at home?" Ninety-nine per cent of the time, they do. Truly, Gunter's nose ... knows.

One of the surprising things about Gunter is that he almost never barks. If we are in the house and someone rings the door bell, he jumps up and runs to the door to investigate, but he seldom makes any vocal sound at all. Our neighbors tell us they appreciate this. In fact, two small dogs in the neighborhood seem to be taking "no-bark" lessons from Gunter. They no longer bark at him; they just smell noses in greeting, and then go on down the street.

People sometimes ask me if Gunter would come to my defense in case of danger. He is not trained as an attack dog, but I believe he would give his life to defend me, if I were threatened. Only one time, in almost three years, I heard him utter a vicious-sounding bark. It was a summer day and the screen door had been left unlocked. An advertising handbill distributor opened our screen door and dropped a pamphlet inside the door when it appeared that there was no one in the house. Like a flash, I heard four loud yelps of warning. Gunter was saying, "You keep away from Marian; I've got big sharp teeth, and I'll give my life to protect her."

A working guide dog is highly educated. Yet the dog will retain a puppy's fun-loving attitude for many years. Gunter has several favorite soft toys which he carries about the house as he moves from room to room. He is not at all destructive. He still has the soft doll his babysitter gave him, and a little knitted mouse that I made when my eyes were still good. Often, when we are at home, he will move to lie down by my chair, bringing along his little mouse and placing it on the floor beside his nose. In pleasant weather he likes to wander out to the screened-in porch, carrying one of his toys with him. Then he will lie down with the toy beside his face, waiting for me to call him to action.

When I wash his toys and pin them on the

clothes line to dry in the sunshine, he watches me carefully. He looks them over, making sure he can see each one in place on the line. It's as though he is calling the roll of his little friends: the squeaking blue heart, his soft doll, his knit mouse, and the little red lion his Aunt Judy gave him. He is concerned about his toys. If he is inside the house, he glances out once in a while just to make sure they are all right. When I go out with him while they are drying, he keeps watch over them, making sure I know that those are his possessions. If I take him out for relief while his toys are hanging on the line, he has to go out past the clothes line for a look at his treasures.

If it seems ridiculous for a grown-up guide dog to cherish his toys, compare this to a grown-up man. For relaxation, a man sticks a worm on a hook and dangles it in the water for hours at a time. Gunter gets his relaxation by playing with his toys.

One thing he never plays with is his food. He is serious about his meals. I try to follow the school's diet recommendations, as well as those of our veterinarian. Gunter gets a mixture of Pedigree Small Crunchy Bites and Purina Fit and Trim, a total of three cups a day. I divide this into two feedings, one in the morning, the second around 3:00 p.m.

We keep his dish of fresh drinking water, always filled, and always in the same place. In hot weather he enjoys having a few ice cubes dropped in the water. Once in a while, especially when temperatures are high, we hear him chewing on his ice.

We try to avoid upsetting Gunter's feeding

schedule. If we go on a trip, we pack little plastic bags of his food mixture to carry along. Each bag contains one feeding of the mixture. Thus, in preparing for a ten-day trip, we must pack twenty little plastic bags of dog food, plus a few extras in case of a delay on the way. We carry these in a small athletic zipper bag. One problem is Gunter's sensitive nose, which always tells him just where his future meals are hidden. In a motel room, we store the bag high above us on a shelf so he isn't tormented by the smell of food close to his nose. We want Gunter to be a happy dog, whether traveling or at home with us.

Once each month he gets his heartworm medicine.

To keep his teeth clean, the veterinarian suggested a smoked knuckle bone for him to chew on. Such a bone can be bought at pet a store. In addition, he gets numerous small doggy-treats, which we give him as rewards. To help keep his weight down, our veterinarian suggested that we break the treats into halves. We are well aware that a guide dog's most valued reward is praise from its master. We try always to be generous in our praise. I remember that one of the trainers at Southeastern said, "If you correct your dog once, you should balance this with 'Good dog' three times."

This is sound advice. I wonder how many human parents follow this plan with their children.

At the dog school we learned that Gunter had received special training for visiting residents of nursing homes. When we go out to play music with our group of two violins and a guitar, we always take Gunter with us. He lies quietly on the floor near us while we play. He never creates any disturbance, never makes any trouble for us. Often when we play in nursing homes, the host will ask me to speak and tell them about guide dogs. When we finish playing, I take off his harness and allow him to make the rounds, shaking hands with members of the audience. It's plain to see by their joyous expressions that Gunter triggers many fond memories of their experiences with their own dogs. Gunter shows by his free kisses and wagging tail that he enjoys every minute of this.

In the public school in our home town, we helped celebrate "American Day." We played for four different elementary classes and demonstrated Gunter's obedience skills. We have taken him to school rooms many times during the two years he has been with us. We have appeared at Lions Club meetings, Rotary Clubs, churches, P.E.O. and Senior Citizens groups.

The Lions Clubs, locally, and all over the country, have given special attention to people with eye problems. A major portion of the financial support for the guide dog programs comes directly from the fund-raising of the Lions Clubs.

Recently we took Gunter with us to a local bank to get an official's signature. The banker said, "I remember you; you and your dog gave a demonstration at our Rotary Club meeting about a year ago."

We visited a Bible school group of more than one hundred young people who were studying how blindness was dealt with in Biblical times, compared with how people handle vision problems today. Gunter demonstrated his obedience skills for them. When I took Gunter out to the grass nearby, we noticed a sheep being pastured in a shady area. The local priest uses many animals in his lessons for young people, right in downtown Tampa Bay. This was Gunter's first experience with a sheep. He got all excited and pranced while I reassured him that everything was all right. The sheep ignored him.

Once when we played for a large crowd at an open house for a retirement home, Gunter was lying down in a dark corner near the wall. He was behind the stage where we were playing. We looked around and noticed an elderly lady lying on the floor beside Gunter. At first we were alarmed, thinking she had fainted or something. Instead, we found that she was playing with Gunter and seemed so happy to be loving him; obviously, it reminded her of playing with her own dog on the floor long ago.

We also take Gunter regularly to make calls for our church. One elderly couple always tell us how glad they are to see Gunter when we take him to visit their apartment. The husband was once a farmer and she a school teacher. They always had dogs on the farm. On one visit, we failed to bring the dog along and they were extremely disappointed. Gunter cheers them up with his warm kisses and wagging tail. She always asks Gunter for a kiss before we leave.

Once we took Gunter into a hospital room to visit a lady who was very ill, too weak to talk so we could understand her. At first she did not know that the dog was with us. When she realized that he was there, she reached out and Gunter put his nose on her hand. Then she began to talk more plainly. We left in a few moments, and we could hear her clearly as she said, "Goodbye, Gunter."

I think we all felt good about this visit.

Gunter's former babysitter, Jill Clark, invited us to bring Gunter to Gainesville to meet four unusual puppy raisers. These were young men who were serving prison sentences, but were now being given the opportunity of raising guide dog puppies for Southeastern. They had never seen a working guide dog until Gunter. While they watched, Gunter demonstrated the way he obeys my commands.

We met in a retirement home; all four men were dressed in white uniforms and one proudly carried a diaper bag containing treats for the dogs. All four dogs assigned to the prisoners were beautiful black Goldadors. The looks on these men's faces showed that were very happy with their dogs. They knew it was an honor to be chosen for this task. As part of this effort to teach responsibility, each man is in charge of his assigned dog for twenty-four hours a day.

The use of prisoners as puppy raisers is a new move by Southeastern. School officials believe that when these dogs are returned to Southeastern for their advanced training, the men will be ready for new guide dog puppies to raise.

A guide dog in training must go through many new experiences. Each person the dog meets makes some contribution to the building of the dog's personality.

We were invited to visit the home of Gunter's puppy raiser near Gainesville. When we drove to the gate of the property we saw a huge green and yellow sign hanging above the entrance. It was made of shiny dark green oil cloth, lettered professionally with the big words, "Welcome Gunter."

When we arrived at the house, Stephanie Gunter came out and the dog greeted her with warm, wet kisses. She had several other dogs and it was easy to see that she is a real dog lover.

I feel that Stephanie did a magnificent job of preparing this dog for his future responsibilities as my guide dog, and I am grateful to her for the part she played in molding his character and making him the loving "person" that he is today.

She told me, "When he was a puppy, I could see that Gunter was always sensitive to peoples' needs." As I observe him today, I can say that he certainly continues with that characteristic. He is always concerned about people and their reactions to him.

One very recent incident that shows his sensitivity: A couple living near us tragically lost their only son. She was talking with me in our back yard while Gunter listened. I was watering the flowers and we walked about several times during our conversation. Each time we moved to a different place, Gunter got up and walked to where he could be as close as possible to the grieving mother.

To show further how sensitive this dog is, we had an experience a few months after he came to live with us. We offered to make accommodations for two girls from a group of touring performers. They would spend three nights in the extra bedroom in our home. I told the placement person on the phone that we had a guide dog in our home, and I would prefer people who were dog lovers. Unfortunately, when the girls came, we found that both had a strong dislike for dogs. Big, friendly Gunter would approach them with wagging tail, and they would scold him in a menacing tone of voice: "Go away, dog!" This rejection hurt him deeply. The girls used the bedroom and took over our living room where Gunter usually greets our guests. I tried to explain to them that this was his home, that they were encroaching on his territory, and that the dog only wanted to be friendly.

Gunter went into hiding in my bedroom, lying on the bed whenever they were around. He showed every sign of a deep depression during the three days they were here.

These were well-behaved girls, college graduates, polite and punctual, nice girls in every other way, but they simply didn't want a dog around. For a friendly dog like Gunter, this was puzzling behavior to understand.

Gunter always follows me around the house, but after these two girls left, I went into their room to change the sheets. When I called Gunter, he would not come into that room. We have frequently had relatives come to visit us, and Gunter has never reacted in this way to them. He knows his friends when he sees them.

After the girls were gone, Gunter was still very quiet and subdued for several days; apparently he was afraid those girls might be coming back. We have decided not to put him through this experience again. Gunter protects us, and we should protect him.

Gunter has always been sensitive to our actions. If we get a suitcase out, he knows immediately that we are getting ready for a trip. His tail wags, and he begins to pant with anticipation, as he smiles broadly and watches every move that we make.

Around the dog school they have a saying: "Each person who graduates thinks that his dog (or her dog) is the very best dog in the school." I heard this saying quoted frequently during my time on campus. And, you know, I have to admit that with me, it's really true! Gunter actually is the best dog in the school.

Here are some of the remarks people make about Gunter:

"Beautiful!"

"Regal!"

"Kingly!" "

"Royal!"

"So clean!"

"You must have just given him a bath."

"Is that a Collie?"

"I've never seen a short-haired Collie."

What can you say about someone else's dog? If you don't know what to say, try this some time. It will help a dog lover go home happy. One lady (whom I did not know) walked up to me in a grocery store and said, "You have a beautiful dog. And you are beautiful, too." This made my day.

One day when we were in the car on a bypass around a city, my husband mistakenly made a U-turn. The blue flashing lights of a state patrolman quickly appeared in the mirror. He asked for my husband's driver's license; then he noticed something else and said,

"Is that a guide dog you have in the back seat?"

"Yes, Sir."

The patrolman said, "I'm familiar with Southeastern Guide Dog School. I was going to give you a ticket, but I can't do that because my parents are puppy raisers for Southeastern, and they wouldn't be happy with me if I ticketed you. So go on, but for your own safety, don't do that again."

Many young mothers must read Ann Landers' newspaper column. She has advised young mothers to tell their children not to pet working dogs, and quite often I hear mothers cautioning their children, "Don't pet that dog. He's a working guide dog." Gunter carries a large red and white sign on his harness, saying, "Do not pet me. I am a working Southeastern Guide Dog." Many times it's not children, but adults who break the rule. They read the sign and go right on to pet him, without even asking permission. Gunter loves them all.

We get so many questions from people in

hotels, restaurants, malls, wherever we go, that my husband decided to do a bit of public relations work for the dog school. He had hundreds of wallet-size color photographs made of Gunter, with lettering on the back telling about the school and the guide dog program. He hands these out to the people, telling them Gunter is a working dog and these are his "business cards." To make up the cards, my husband has to do a lot of hand work, cutting out a printed text just the right size to stick on the back of each photo. He jokes that he is glad he did so well in kindergarten, cutting out paper dollies, which qualified him for this work.

People seem very grateful for the photos; some want to give them to their grandchildren for "show and tell;" others say, "Oh, is this for me? Thank you." In our small town, sometimes we hear this response: "Thank you, I already have a picture of Gunter on my refrigerator at home." One local restaurant displays Gunter's picture near the cash register where people pay their bills. The manager tells them that the dog is one customer who never complains.

When we go on vacation trips, many of Gunter's "business cards" are distributed.

Once on a Caribbean cruise, the passengers played a game called scavenger hunt. The audience was divided into five sections. There was a request for "a picture of a dog," and five of these little photos of Gunter were brought up to the stage.

Often we notice small children who become all excited about seeing a dog. For example, in a restaurant, a tiny little boy in a high chair kept shouting, "Gag, gag!" I didn't realize that he was trying to say "Dog." After I finished my meal I took Gunter down to this family's table, and sure enough, this was what the little child had been saying. The parents thanked me profusely for taking the trouble to let the little boy see the dog.

I recognize that people have a genuine interest in guide dogs, but they don't know where to turn for information. For example, we were attending a meeting in a St. Louis hotel where a group of McDonnell-Douglass executives were standing on a mezzanine. They could look down and see us with the dog, where we sat by the pool below. As the men talked among themselves about guide dogs, they decided to leave their party and come down to see if I would tell them about my dog. I invited them to sit down. They were there about ten minutes, asking very intelligent questions about the guide dog program. This was one of the reasons we decided to make up the "business cards" with Gunter's photograph. We feel that wherever there is an interest, we should provide the information.

Here is the text that goes on the back of the photograph:

"My name is Gunter. I am a smooth-coat Collie. I obey 40 commands. I enjoy my work. In every state, with my visually impaired partner, I have legal access to hotels, taxis, buses, airplanes, malls, stores, restaurants. If you'd like to help train more guide dogs contact SOUTHEASTERN GUIDE DOGS, 4210 77th St. E., Palmetto, FL 34221 (941) 729-5665."

One time we had a gathering of our family in a Holiday Inn. Gunter and I were sitting in a lunch room visiting with our children. I heard an unfamiliar voice, so I felt I should check on Gunter, who was on the floor beside me. There was a strange man, down on all fours, talking to Gunter. Red-faced and embarrassed, he immediately apologized, saying, "I love dogs." Later, our daughter told us she had seen an I.D. tag on the man's jacket: Manager.

Once we were eating in another crowded restaurant. The hostess came and asked permission to seat another couple with us at our table. After talking with the people for a few minutes, we found that they were deeply troubled because their daughter, who was a school teacher in the Midwest, was losing her eyesight. The daughter had expressed an interest in getting a guide dog, but had no idea who to contact or how to go about it. We were very happy to tell them all we knew.

As we parted, the mother grasped my hand and said, "I'm so happy we got to meet you; the Holy Spirit works in strange ways."

Perhaps the Spirit led another man and wife who came up to us and asked all sorts of questions about the guide dog program. He said he had worked for the same insurance company since he was eighteen.

"Now, in retirement," he said, "we like to help with good projects. Those pension checks keep coming every month and I want my money to go for worthy causes."

We wonder if he felt he had now found a worthy charity to help.

While we were eating in a busy cafeteria, a

couple came up to us and asked us about Gunter. The lady was visually impaired. She told us they had just had to retire the golden retriever guide dog she had had for eleven years. We expressed sympathy, because this must have been a tragic episode for her at this time. She told me that she had graduated from Southeastern when Mike Sergeant had just started the school. At that time there were only three in her class. She was happy that the school is growing so rapidly.

One day, a waitress at a fast food restaurant along the Interstate came to our table and started asking me questions about Gunter. She explained that her son-in-law had recently lost his eyesight and was very discouraged about his future. She asked us if we would send her information about guide dogs, which we did, giving her the phone number and address of the school.

It seems to me that Gunter opens the door of understanding for people who are concerned about their vision problems. When they see Gunter leading me, they can picture themselves, or their loved ones, being led by a trained guide dog.

Through Gunter, we have met many people who are curious about the problems of those with failing vision. His presence invites friendly conversation.

There can be no question that Gunter enjoys his work.

When we say something about "go" -- "go" for a walk, for a ride in the car, whatever, Gunter's ears perk up, his tail wags, and he pants with excitement. Then he always goes to where his harness hangs on the wall, waiting for me to put it on him. His collar has three tags: rabies inoculation, Southeastern Guide Dogs, and Zephyrhills city license. As he moves about in the house, I can tell where he is by the musical sound of his tags rattling.

For his own comfort, we always take him out for relief before we go anywhere.

When we go to the window of a drive-up bank, Gunter is sitting on the back seat of our car. He puts his two front paws on the arm rest between us on the front seat so he can be ready for the treat that he knows the clerk will send out to him. His mouth waters with anticipation while he waits. He remembers that he always gets a treat there.

At home, when he hears the refrigerator door open, he rushes up for one of his favorite treats: he likes cold, uncooked baby carrots which we hand to him one at a time. Our local veterinarian suggested this, and Gunter has given his full approval.

We have traveled many thousands of miles since Gunter came to live with us. Our first automobile trip with him was 2,500 miles, and he proved to be a perfect traveler. He has the back seat of our car all to himself, with a bowl of water accessible to him. He often sits on his haunches and rests his chin on the back of the seat so he can look around. Most of the time, he sleeps all stretched out on a big bath towel spread across the back seat.

We have found that most of the fast food restaurants along the highways have grassy spots where a dog can be relieved. He always looks as though he fully enjoys these rest stops. He likes to sniff the scents that have been left behind by other dogs. I take off his harness and use his long leash to give him more freedom of movement.

For our overnight stops, we always choose motels that have grassy areas surrounding them. If they don't have grass, we drive on. We get a room with two double beds and I carry a sheet along to spread over Gunter's bed. My husband tells the registration clerk that we have a guide dog with us. This has never created a problem.

At one motel, the lady in charge came out and asked if she could see the dog; she said she couldn't wait "to see the puppy." Obviously, she was a real dog lover.

When we stop along the way, we offer Gunter fresh drinking water. We are careful in hot weather to avoid letting him walk long distances over burning hot sidewalks.

We stopped for lunch one day at a Holiday Inn restaurant. The waitress brought a pan of water and placed it under the table for Gunter. Then she asked us if she could bring him a steak-bone and a plate of cold cuts. While we truly appreciated her thoughtfulness, we had to decline and tell her that he is never fed from the table. I remember one waitress in a fast food place who brought a hamburger and laid it on the table, saying, "This is for your dog. It's on the house."

Recently, we visited a beach restaurant. As we walked in, the hostess said, "You've been here before; about a year ago." Then she looked at the dog, and said, "And your name is Gunter."

When we finish eating in a restaurant, Gunter can lead me back to where the car is parked. I simply say, "Gunter, find the car," and he takes me right to it. Obviously, there are limits to this skill; I can't expect him to find our car in the parking lots at Busch Gardens, but he can find it at church. After he locates the car, I say, "Gunter, find the door." He always goes to the right rear door. Then I say, "Find the knob." His nose goes directly to the handle of the car door.

A reminder from the trainers at the dog school: When you are seated in a restaurant, with the dog under the table, it's only fair to warn the waitress that the dog is there. Too many times, a waitress can be startled when she sees a dog in an unexpected place, and it could be dangerous if she is carrying hot coffee.

I have noticed that if people's backs are turned as we come in, they make a startled sound when they see the dog where they don't usually see one.

If there is a hostess, we often request seating beside a wall or window, to give plenty of room for the dog. This keeps him from being in the flow of traffic, where he might get his tail or a foot stepped on. We try to give him plenty of room, since he is larger than many guide dogs. However, he willingly goes under the table in the usual way if I ask him to.

In a fast food restaurant, my husband does the ordering while Gunter and I find a place to settle. I have found that, in most McDonalds, there is a little more room for the dog in the seating near the restroom area.

Because we know the sensitivity of a dog's nose, Harold and I seldom eat our fast food in the car with Gunter. It would be torment for him to inhale all the delicious smells of a hamburger inside the car, and never get a taste for his own enjoyment.

Most of the newer fast food restaurants have restrooms with large stalls for the handicapped. These are very helpful when I go with the dog into the rest room.

Air travel is no problem with Gunter. We took him on a small privately owned jet which had only a little boarding ladder, so we had to help him climb on board. Once inside, he lay comfortably in the aisle, near the front of the aircraft. We noticed that the pilot and co-pilot frequently reached back to pet the dog during the flight. They both said that they loved dogs, and had tried to find a blanket to make him comfortable.

On the commercial airlines there are different methods of handling a guide dog at the security check. Some require the harness to be removed; others use a scanner to go over his body. All the security personnel are very kind to the dog and to me, making it as simple as possible. None of them seem to resent a dog coming through; it probably makes a pleasant break for those who are dog lovers.

One time on a commercial flight, the flight attendant came to meet us as we boarded. She had been notified in advance that there would be a guide dog aboard. She said,

"We have plenty of room on this flight in First Class; we'll just change you to that class." A grandson, Kevin, traveling with us, got to enjoy a steak dinner instead of peanuts.

On other flights, we have found that the dog has more space if we request seating just behind the bulkhead. He lies quietly at our feet. Because of his training, he ignores our meal when food is served. On takeoffs and landings, if the changes in pressure bother him, he never shows any discomfort. We have always been treated very well by the flight crews. It seems to me that they enjoy the unique experience of having a guide dog aboard. Flight crews and other passengers often compliment us on Gunter's good behavior.

Once we are on the ground again, we disembark and then walk. We feel that the dog benefits from the exercise of the long walks necessary in some airports. (So do we). In fact, we prefer to walk rather than ride on those long "people movers" that look like horizontal escalators.

In the big St. Louis airport a pilot was walking beside us. He was praising Gunter's fine behavior and regal appearance. I asked him if he knew of a grassy area where we could take the dog for relief. He seemed surprised, and said,

"Now that you mention it, I don't believe there is such a place here." Then he suggested a place where we might go outside, and there we found a couple of bushes.

When we travel by air, we are sometimes frustrated to see how often a new airline employee is put on the job without any information at all about guide dogs. For one example, my husband phoned one carrier to reserve space on a flight from Tampa to St. Louis. He mentioned that I would have a guide dog traveling with me. The novice reservation clerk said,

"Of course, the dog will travel in a crate with the luggage." My husband said,

"Oh, no, the guide dog travels right with my wife in the passenger cabin." She said,

"Let me check." After a long wait, she came back on the line and meekly agreed,

"The dog travels in the passenger cabin."

We have never had an instance of discourteous treatment by airline personnel. They show every interest in helping to make our travel pleasant.

If we are making a long flight and changing planes, we have learned to notify the airline people ahead of time that we will need help in finding a "doggy relief" area. One example, in Pittsburgh, the only accessible grassy spot is at one end of the big terminal, beyond the luggage claim area. The airline brought one of those electric carts to move us easily. Gunter climbed aboard without difficulty, but on the first ride, they placed him on the back platform where his rear feet kept slipping off. It could have been very dangerous for him, with those electric carts zipping around the crowded terminal. After that, we learned to ask for a place on the electric cart where there would be enough room for the dog to stand. Or he could have ridden sitting up on the seat. We usually have to make those decisions in a great hurry, with all of the airport bustle going on. We learn from our experiences.

One time at Pittsburgh, a heavy rainstorm was going on when we approached the grassy area. Gunter hates to get his feet wet. But, true to his obedience training, he walked bravely out into the rain and stood on the wet grass while he took care of his personal needs.

In our second year with Gunter, we discovered that an ocean cruise is a good way for us to travel. Happily for me, Ed Eyre, a travel agent from Stuart, Florida, and a graduate of Southeastern, began putting together cruises that include people with guide dogs. The trips are operated as fund-raisers, to bring in money for the school. He has a beautiful yellow Labrador named Andie. In cooperation with Holland America Lines, he arranged for guide dogs to be welcomed on their cruises.

To join the cruise, the people with guide dogs rode a bus from the school near Palmetto to Ft. Lauderdale. Our first cruise was on the Westerdam. When we got out of the bus, officials from Holland

America met us, offering to help us fill out the necessary papers; then they ushered us past the waiting crowd straight to the elevators to board the ship. Then they turned us over to an escort, who took us to our pleasant cabin with a king sized bed.

After we got settled in, we decided to go look for the dogs' relief area. We found that Ed had already chosen a secluded deck, down a couple of floors from our rooms. This area was inelegantly called the poop deck. Gunter had no problem adjusting to the use of either smooth wooden decks or painted metal decks, instead of his favorite grass. Now, I understand that Southeastern is training dogs to relieve themselves on concrete in addition to their grass relief training. Of course, on shipboard, we all try to be environmentally correct. We carry plastic bags to pick up all droppings, depositing them in trash buckets and never tossing them overboard. The ship's crew hoses down the decks several times a day.

One thing that impressed me was the friendliness of the Indonesian crew members on the ship. Once they had learned Gunter's name, he was like an old friend to them. They would greet us at the diningroom door, calling Gunter by name as we entered.

One day as I was walking down a beautiful curved stairway on the ship, I was hanging onto the railing with my right hand as I always do. One of the crew members, wishing to be friendly, shouted, "Hello, Gunter!" He repeated it several times. This could have caused the dog to hesitate, resulting in a bad fall for me. It's a good illustration of why guide dogs should not be interfered with when they are working. I gave Gunter the command, "Forward," and he obeyed me, so all was well.

Several of us with guide dogs gave a demonstration of our dogs' skills before a crowd of some two hundred guests on the Westerdam, and answered many questions. One volunteer for the dog school, to end the program, mentioned that Southeastern never turns anyone away because of lack of money, if the person needs a dog. This fact is important to know.

Gunter, Harold and I, the three of us, had such a good time on this cruise that we decided to go on another, on the Statendam. Soon after we got on board, I was surprised when one of the Indonesian crew members shouted, "Hello, Gunter!" I asked him how he knew the dog's name and he replied that he had been on the previous cruise with us, on the Westerdam.

On this cruise, the entertainment director invited people with guide dogs to put on a program for those who were interested. To our amazement, the theater was almost full. We all came out with our dogs and sat on the large stage. The program began with a showing of the movie "Yaz," the story of Elisha Gilliland and her guide dog. As the master of ceremonies introduced each of us, with our dogs, the dogs lay quietly at the feet of their masters.

All but Gunter! When his name was called, he rose slowly on his long white legs, looked about the auditorium with his ears up, and took a big bow before lying back down. He got an enthusiastic burst of applause.

Cruise ships provide really fine entertainment which is presented each night of the cruise. We found that Gunter enjoyed watching and listening, so we attended every night, choosing seats close to the front so I could make out the forms of the people on the stage. On this trip there was a highly professional Spanish flamenco dance team who used loud castanets in their routine. After a few minutes of the rhythmic clacking, we could tell that the sound was bothering Gunter's ears. He was restlessly getting up and lying back down, shifting his position constantly. He behaved for all the world like a man with a splitting headache. We quietly left the auditorium. Later that same evening as we strolled about the ship, we encountered these same dancers. My husband began apologizing to them for walking out on their performance, but found that they felt a need to apologize to us for disturbing Gunter. During the friendly conversation, the dancers stated that they, too, were dog lovers. They showed us pictures of their own dogs and we parted friends.

We smile about how Gunter gets royal treatment on a cruise ship, in keeping with his regal appearance. In the diningroom, waiters greet him by name and assist us to find our seats. He lies on the floor at my feet. A person who did not see us come in would never know he is present. If we choose to eat in the ship's bountiful buffet, Gunter walks slowly with us as we fill our trays, then a polite waiter tells me what items of food are available for me to put on my tray. We follow the waiter who finds a vacant table for us. They usually seat us at a table near an observation window with a carpeted ledge for Gunter to lie on. He thrives on all the attention he gets from waiters and from other passengers. Friends and acquaintances come by to greet him and it is as though "His Royal Highness" is holding court in the buffet.

On the stop at Caracas, Venezuela, my husband was determined to go looking for cashew nuts. He recalled a trade mission to Venezuela which he had made many years before, when he traveled as a reporter with the U.S. Secretary of Agriculture, John R. Block. My husband remembered that the cashew nuts he sampled at a reception in Caracas were the best he had ever tasted.

We arranged for Gunter's "grandma," Betty Crowell, to baby-sit with him on the ship while we went ashore to look for cashew nuts. On shore, in a crowded shopping area, my husband spoke Spanish and asked, "Donde se puede comprar nueces de cashew?" The clerk replied, "Mas alla!" Farther away. It turned out the clerk was talking about tin cans of "Planters" cashew nuts in a super market, just like those we could have bought in the States. So we went back to the ship without any Venezuelan cashews.

When we got back on board, Betty and Barbara were sitting on deck chairs with Gunter beside them. My husband said Gunter's ears went up as he watched us approaching. Betty, a smoker, said that Gunter had told them he disapproved of their smoking, so they didn't use cigarettes while he was with them. I said, "What did he say that made you think he didn't like your smoking?" Betty held her nose high in the air and closed her eyes to imitate his actions.

At some of the ports where the ship stopped, we chose not to go ashore. We had visited most of those places before. We remembered seeing wild dogs running loose in some countries, and we decided not to subject Gunter to this. However, some of the other people with dogs took them ashore and got along fine. Perhaps time had improved the conditions there.

On both cruise ships, we noticed that Gunter never made a mistake in finding our room. The doors all looked alike to Harold, except for the different numbers on the front. But Gunter could pick out our room from the rest. He would walk confidently up to the door, give it a good sniff, and turn to Harold as if to say, "This is your room; can't you tell?"

Gunter helps us make friends with the other passengers on a cruise. As we say goodbye, we notice that everyone remembers Gunter by name, even though they may not remember our names.

One travel option that is less expensive than a cruise is a visit to a state park. It is one of our favorite places, and we know that Gunter likes it too. He loves the scenic boardwalks that are found in many of the Florida parks. He walks along, leading me joyously, his toenails clicking along the weathered boards. He totally ignores saucy squirrels that occasionally stare at us from a nearby tree.

When he sees something unusual or different, Gunter has a way of prancing. I can feel this in my left hand as we walk along. It makes it seem that he is walking on his tiptoes. He sees all of the rabbits and birds along the walkways, but he never tries to give chase. It's almost as though he is saying to us, "Look at that frog!" Or "See that flock of ducks!"

On his first visit to a state park with us, a ranger yelled from a distance, "Get out of there with that dog; can't you see the sign, 'No pets allowed?'" My husband yelled back politely, "Sir, this is no pet; it's a working guide dog." The ranger's attitude changed completely as he apologized and told us to enjoy our day in the park.

Harold and I are both thankful for Gunter's sunny disposition, and for the way his presence adds pleasure to our travels.

I am amazed at this dog's ability to concentrate totally on the task before him. Once at a convention of people with guide dogs, Gunter and I were walking toward an open door where several dogs were standing. One irritable young German Shepherd guide dog rushed up to Gunter with a vicious growl. I felt my dog go into his prancing walk. My husband watched as Gunter led me on calmly, paying absolutely no attention to the growling Shepherd, as though to say, "Keep away from me, Kid, can't you see I'm working?"

Much has been written about the bond of love that grows ever stronger between a human and a dog. In the case of an impaired person, greatly dependent upon the dog, the bond is even stronger than it is with a person and a pet. Most pet dogs are left at home for many hours every day, but most guide dogs and other service animals spend their days and nights close by the side of their masters. For this reason, I know that I am more closely bonded to Gunter than I could ever be to any canine who is "just a pet dog." Gunter and I are deeply dependent upon one another, and that bond is enhanced by our love for one another.

I am astonished to find that I can overhear many of the comments people are making when I walk by with Gunter. Never anything derogatory, the comments are usually shared by people within hearing distance of where I am walking. Often the comments are directed at me, telling me that they think my dog is beautiful.

"What a beautiful dog!" is probably the most frequently heard comment.

When we go into a restaurant and find our seats, I sometimes overhear other patrons as their conversation turns to the subject of dogs. Many recall some fond memory of a happy experience they had long ago with a dog, and the sight of a guide dog entering the restaurant triggers this memory.

One kind-hearted lady said to me,

"When I saw you with your dog, I knew that I was seeing an angel; that was your guardian angel walking along beside you."

Among the frequently heard questions:

"What kind of a dog is that? I've never seen one like that." "Is that a greyhound nose?"

"Oh, did you just give him a bath?"

"Did you just have him sheared?"

"Oh, he's got two different colored eyes!"

"Can he see out of both eyes?"

"My, he's a big dog; you should be riding him."

"I have a cookie here; may I give it to him?"

Sometimes they don't ask; they just hand him

treats.

Once at a dinner my husband noticed his seating partner slipping french fries to Gunter under the table. Not wishing to offend the man, my husband waited, and then finally laid his hand gently on the man's arm and said, "We're really not supposed to feed a guide dog from the table." The man nodded in reply. A few minutes later, my husband saw him slipping the dog another french fry.

At a buffet, a lady came by with a big bone on her plate and asked me, "May I give your dog this bone?" Her intentions were so good--it hurt me to tell her that I had to decline her offer with thanks.

When we arrived at a Tampa restaurant another customer asked,

"What kind of dog is that?"

I said, "It's a smooth coat Collie."

As we were leaving the same restaurant, after eating, the same man was still there. He smiled and said, "That's so-o-ome slick Collie."

Our daughter, Debby Snider, shares several memories. She writes, "I like to look at the December video of Gunter. Your fine Christmas trinkets on the coffee table are softly knocked over as Gunter's tail swoops in its usual happy rhythm. He doesn't even notice.

"He greatly impressed me in Key Largo, when he rode with us down the canal in a small boat. Like a sea captain, he observed both sides of the water's edge, never flinching, as the braying, possessive resident dogs gave him 'What-for.' His attitude seemed to say, 'What are you trying to prove--that you are a dog?'"

Each year Debby teaches a high school class in which the students receive college credit. Her letter continues,

"My first college credit English class was a very large group—30 students. One of our first writing activities required that the students compose a narrative. When people of high school age are asked to remember their pasts, they often turn to their beloved pets—or former pets—as subjects. Later, reading the compositions aloud, the students observed that over half were dog stories. As we listened to stories of puppy tricks, destructive canine surprises, and lingering deaths, we animal-lovers went through a range of emotions. I couldn't resist telling the students about my mother's guide dog. I explained how much he had done to restore Mom's independence, and what he meant to the whole family. The talk drifted, then, to an incredible lawsuit being filed in Florida. A mall walker was suing the dog training school for injuries allegedly caused by the step of a seeing eye dog. What an injustice! What an outrage! All of us agreed that the lawsuit was preposterous.

"The subject of dogs had brought up many feelings.

"Since that day, I have used that legal case as an introduction to the 'argumentation essay' assignment. When some of my students say that there is no major issue that they feel like arguing, this event is a subject to discuss. All agree that visually impaired people and their dogs deserve their rights. Now the students have a topic about which they feel strongly.

"Years fly by in the career of an English teacher. Many, many essays pass one's desk. Graduates join adult society. However, some things that have been said or done at school can remain in the minds of the individual students. In July, of 1996, when Mother, Gunter and I visited my local bank, I was reminded of that fact. Mother was talking to the bank official, with Gunter by her side. I happened to notice that two of my former students, several years apart in age, had come into the bank. They came and went separately; they probably didn't even know each other. When each one saw Gunter, she pointed, let her mouth drop, smiled, and met my eyes as if to say, 'That's the guide dog you told us about.'"

Debby's letter concludes, "To paraphrase a famous quote, we never know where our influence stops. Gunter has an influence over others. Without complaint, he does his duties every day; he works with confidence. He equally serves as a model of what many people have never seen in action--a true working dog. With his beautiful coat, tall stature, and neat leather harness, he attracts attention. Onlookers often ask questions about him. But many others watch, observe his abilities, yet do not utter a sound. These silent individuals are influenced. And then, there are people like my students, who have never seen a working dog, but only heard about one. They, too, are influenced. Gunter changes perceptions. Wherever he goes, he is a lesson in life. People touched by Gunter may one day need a working dog themselves, or advise a loved one that such dogs can improve lives. He does extraordinary work. He has tremendous influence."

As soon as we received this letter from Debby, we phoned to ask her permission to include it in this book about Gunter, which she graciously gave us.

Our grandson, Chad Sellmer, has researched one of the oldest dog training programs in the country: Guide Dogs for the Blind, San Rafael, CA. This school has an additional campus at Boring, OR. It currently serves about 1,550 graduates of a program that matches guide dogs with visually impaired partners. The school was established in 1942, to serve blind veterans of World War Two. As a news reporter for the Novato Advance, Chad visited the San Rafael campus and reports that through the years Guide Dogs for the Blind has graduated close to 8,000 guide dogs and their blind partners.

Like Southeastern and other such training facilities, this school is a tax-exempt, non-profit organization. This means it receives no government aid or corporate funding of any kind. Each visually impaired person who goes through the intensive training program -- 28 days in a dormitory setting with the dog -- is provided with all necessary equipment and training at no cost to the participant.

Chad interviewed Morry Angell, a spokesperson at the San Rafael school. She told him everything is done through private donations. She went on to acknowledge the Lion's Club as a big supporter, with most of the donations coming from individuals.

Angell told Chad they always have about 300

dogs on campus being trained. A dog spends as much as 30 months in training, before it is ready to be matched with its human partner. Only about half of the puppies who begin training make it to become successful guide dogs. Those that don't "graduate" may find work as breeders for future guide dogs.

At San Rafael, the more popular guide dog breeds include Labrador retrievers (both black and yellow), German Shepherds, and Golden retrievers.

The school's capacity is 24 human-and-canine teams per month. Participants live in two-person dormitory rooms, each with his or her dog. They spend their time learning to work together and forming a bond as the human partner learns to trust the dog's sight in place of their own.

The end result is a happy team which has learned to live and work together.

Chad noted that the program is undergirded by a dedicated group of volunteers. He says the volunteers give up an average of 20 hours per week, as well as giving up a little bit of their hearts, to raise and help socialize the puppies during their first formative years.

Chad interviewed Kathleen Seaman of Novato, CA., a 4-H Club guide dog project leader. She helps match puppies from the school with puppy-raisers in the area who have a yard and are willing to work closely with the dogs. Sometimes this involves more than a year. All the while, the puppy raisers are aware that they will have to give up the puppy when it is placed with its visually impaired human partner. Seaman told Chad that the puppies, during this time, are expected to learn the basics like housebreaking, obedience and manners with their assigned puppy-raiser.

The raiser usually takes the puppy at about 6 to 8 weeks of age and sees it through its first 12 to 18 months, helping the growing dog to socialize and become familiar with a wide variety of human situations.

All of the puppy raisers are volunteers, and it's estimated that each one puts in a minimum of one thousand hours a year to raise one puppy. Some of the volunteers are adults, and some are 4-H youngsters. The puppy raisers range in age from 10 to 70.

The different dog training schools have various ways of handling the puppy raising program, but they all have one thing in common. Once the puppy has become a part of the family, it's always very hard to give it up when the time comes for the puppy to go back to the school. The attachments which have been formed are a part of the growing-up experience for the puppy. When the time comes, it's necessary for the puppy to move on to a new life. It's like sending a human child off to college, and then after graduation, seeing it married to a new partner.

The sadness of saying goodbye to the grown-up puppy is tempered by the joy of welcoming a new cuddly puppy to the home. Guide dog puppy raisers feel that, if the puppy doesn't form an attachment to them, the grown-up dog is not going to form an attachment to its new partner.

Bonding is very important to the dog's future success as a working guide dog. Volunteers find that, even ten years after a puppy has left their home, the grown-up dog still remembers them. Experienced puppy raisers know that each dog has its own individual personality, so it's never hard to remember which dog is which.

At the beginning of the guide dog movement, German Shepherds were predominant among the breeds trained for this work. In later years trainers experimented with Labradors, Golden Retrievers, Australian Shepherds, Hungarian Vizslas, Boxers, and smooth-coat Collies. Not surprisingly, each breed has its own advocates, pushing for its acceptance and increased use as guide dogs.

Gunter was among several smooth-coat Collies trained at the time I was in school at Southeastern. His short hair makes him easier to care for than a long-haired dog. He still requires daily brushing and grooming, but for a person with failing eyesight, the time occupied in caring for him is not as great as with a long-haired breed.

Someone said to me, "Did you just give your dog a haircut?" I happily responded, "No, he never needs a haircut."

The Collie breeders who raised Gunter's father are Allene and Tom McKewen of Lakeland, Florida. They point out that the smooth-coat Collie is easy to care for, yet it inherits the intelligence for which the Collie is noted.

Gunter is a living, loving, example of that. Each day I thank God for the blessings Gunter brings me.

FIDELCO GUIDE DOG FOUNDATION, INC. (1981) P.O. BOX 142, Bloomfield, CT 06002 (203) 243-5200

GUIDE DOG FOUNDATION FOR THE BLIND, INC. (1948) 371 East Jericho Turnpike, Smithtown, NY 11787 (515) 265-2121

GUIDE DOGS FOR THE BLIND, INC. (1942) P.O. Box 1200, San Rafael, CA 94915 (415) 479-4000

GUIDE DOGS OF THE DESERT, INC. (1972) P.O. Box 1692, Palm Springs, CA 92263 (619) 329-6257

GUIDING EYES FOR THE BLIND, INC. (1956) 611 Granite Springs Road, Yorktown Heights, NY 10598 (914) 245-4024

GUIDE DOGS OF AMERICA (1948) 13445 Glenoaks Blvd., Sylmar, CA 91342 (800) 528-2552 or (800) 824-9762

LEADER DOGS FOR THE BLIND (1939) 1039 South Rochester Road, Rochester, MI 48063 (810) 651-0911

PILOT DOGS, INC. (1950) 625 West Town Street, Columbus, OH, 43215 (614) 221-6367

THE SEEING EYE, INC.   (1929)   P.O. Box 375, Morristown, NJ, 07960 (201) 539-4425

SOUTHEASTERN GUIDE DOGS, INC. (1982)   4210 77th Street East, Palmetto, FL 34221   (941) 729-5665

I had never seen a Collie working as a guide dog until my husband and I began our volunteer work at Southeastern Guide Dogs, Inc. And I had never seen a smooth-coat Collie before. I didn't even know there was such a thing. At the time we began helping as exercisers at the dog school, they had several smooth Collies in training. We quickly fell in love with them because of their friendly disposition. We liked their neat appearance and the ease of grooming them. Some of the smooth Collies in training were fawn and white; others were tri-colors, and blue Merles. And among the smooth Collies in training at this time was this big, beautiful Gunter, whom we came to know and love.

I still feel that I could have learned to love any breed of guide dog that was matched to me in my training. But after my happy experience with Gunter, I have to say that he is special. He is, without a doubt, the perfect guide dog for me.

Tom and Allene McKewen of Lakeland, Florida, are the breeders behind Gunter and the other Collies at Southeastern Guide Dog School. Gunter's sire was Ch Olympus, from a prize-winning Collie line called Burnished Brass.

Allene is widely known as an artist, renowned for her illustrations of Collies. She produced breed standard illustrations for the Smooth Collie breed. Her interest in Smooth Collies goes back many years, to when she was associated with Dr. Lee Ford's

Shamrock Research Group in Butler, Indiana. Dr. Ford was a pioneer in the breeding of smooth Collies for use as guide dogs.

After Mike and Jan Sergeant founded Southeastern Guide Dogs at Palmetto, Florida, Allene got in touch with the Sergeants to suggest that they consider adding smooth Collies to the breeds in use at Southeastern. Mike had worked with Collies years before, and the Puppy Program Supervisor, Julie Aichroth, had also had experience with them in guide dog work. They were interested, because Southeastern endeavors to produce a variety of dogs to match the varied personalities of the humans they serve. What's more, they wanted a dog that was highly intelligent, and one that would do well in a southern climate.

Southeastern began with a highly successful smooth Collie named Lancer, from Allene McKewen's breeding. Lancer's success was followed within a few months by other smooth-coat Collies taking their place successfully in the force of working dogs being turned out by Southeastern. Allene glows with pride as she hears how well the smooth-coats are doing. She avoids saying, "I told you so." But she adds this note about the Collie as a guide dog:

"The Collie is perfect, the best in the field."

She goes on to point out that it takes a unique person to understand and develop the full potential of a Collie. If the person is too demanding, too restrictive, too dominant, or too critical, the Collie will quit. She quotes a trainer at Southeastern as saying that he simply puts the Collie in a position to learn --- AND LETS HIM !

Allene had the privilege of working closely with the Southeastern trainers on the Collie project. She pointed out to them that if the person is truly in tune with his dog partner, the Collie is perfect. She says that blind people need a dog that will say, "No, you can't proceed because there is danger." They need a dog who can make a decision when a new situation arises.

For those persons interested in word origins, we look back many centuries to the Gaelic tribes that first settled on the British Isles. To those sturdy pioneers, the word Collie simply meant "useful." So a COLLIE dog was a useful dog.

The early Victorian period in England was the high point for the Smooth coated Collie. Princess Victoria became Queen of England in 1837. She was a great admirer of the Smooth coated Collie.

While the Dalmatian was the most famous carriage dog of that time, the Smooth coated Collie became the carriage dog of fashionable ladies. The Dalmatian walked along beside the carriage; the Smooth Collie rode in the carriage.

A British expert on Smooth Collies, Iris Combe, notes in her history that the early Victorian period was the heyday of the "elegant, faithful Smooth coated Collie."

When British breeders began keeping records, the earliest Smooth coated Collie recorded was Sharp, born in 1864. This dog was the constant companion of Queen Victoria for more than 15 years. A statue marks his grave in Windsor Home Park, speaking eloquently of the Queen's love for this canine.

That is as far as I care to explore into the pedigrees of Smooth coated Collies, but we know that they figured prominently in the blood lines of dogs owned by British royalty.

In our three years of acquaintance with Smooth-coated Collies, we have found that very few people have even heard of them. As I've mentioned earlier, this is one reason we distribute Gunter's picture on his business cards, identifying him as a Smooth-coat Collie.

Southeastern Guide Dog School, I think, is making a wise choice in using a variety of breeds for training as guide dogs. I can see that a hard-pulling, fast-stepping, powerful dog would not be ideal for me. I have often referred to Gunter as a gentle giant, and that is exactly what I need for a guide dog.

Southeastern was founded in 1982, in a house trailer set among the orange groves near Palmetto, Florida. In addition, the school now has a downtown training branch at Bradenton. Expanded facilities at the campus let them house 100 adult dogs in training. They have a goal of graduating 200 guide dog teams per year by the year 2000. The addition of a Puppy Kennel allows an increase in their breeding program.

With the hands-on, personal attention which Mike and Jan Sergeant give to the operation of Southeastern, and with the dedication I have observed in the many persons concerned with the school, I feel that their success will continue.

When we talk to other people about Gunter, we often use the generic term, "seeing eye dog", because the name is so widely understood and accepted. In the strict sense of the term, the only "seeing eye" dogs are those graduated by the School of the Seeing Eye, Inc., at Morristown, New Jersey.

Those of us who depend upon guide dogs today are greatly indebted to those pioneers who started the Seeing Eye movement in the 1920's and '30's.

At the end of World War One the German military experimented around Potsdam with the use of specially trained dogs as guides for soldiers who had been blinded in the war.

In the 1920's an article appeared in a U.S. magazine, the Saturday Evening Post, about an effort in Switzerland to train dogs to guide the blind. The article was written by an American widow living in Switzerland, Mrs. Dorothy Eustis. It came to the attention of a recently blinded young man in Nashville, Tennessee, Morris Frank. He was grieving the loss of his sight from a freak boxing accident which had cut short his career as an insurance salesman.

"If I could only get one of those dogs, I could go back to work," he reasoned. "A dog guide would give me back my mobility."

He wrote to Mrs. Eustis and showed such enthusiasm that she invited him to come to

Switzerland and begin training with a female German Shepherd named Buddy.

Working with a skilled trainer, Jack Humphrey, Mrs. Eustis succeeded in molding Morris Frank and Buddy into a smooth-working human-canine team. On completion of the training, Morris Frank returned to Nashville in high spirits, eager to resume his insurance career.

But even before he reached Nashville, Morris Frank ran into trouble. The American public of 1937 did not accept the idea of dogs going on buses or trains. On the train trip, from New York to Nashville, Morris Frank was forced to ride in the baggage car with his dog. In Nashville, taxicab drivers refused to carry the dog. Morris was ordered out of restaurants when he tried to bring the dog inside. In Nashville as he waited at bus stops, drivers shouted coldly through the door, "No dogs allowed on this bus."

When the young insurance representative succeeded in making a sale, the customer often added some degrading remark such as, "I bought the policy because I like your dog. Bring the dog back to see me any time."

Frank went to the existing organizations which were set up to help the blind, asking them to put on public demonstrations so that he could show what Buddy could do. They turned him down, saying, "For years we've been trying to do away with the image of the blind beggar with his tin cup and his dog."

Another remark, "It's bad enough being blind,

without being tied to a dog."

It took much effort to get the public attention he needed. After his dog pulled him from a burning automobile at a crash scene, the Nashville Banner ran a feature article about Morris Frank and his dog. This brought the first significant attention to the use of guide dogs for the blind.

In Switzerland, Mrs. Eustis had decided she would not return to the United States until she could come home with a purpose. When she heard of Morris Frank's success with Buddy, she said, "Now I have found my purpose: to start a school for dogs to lead the blind." She came to Nashville and working together with Morris Frank, began a school to train dogs and their visually impaired partners, which she named "The Seeing Eye." Many people came for training with the dogs, and the school grew. But because of Nashville's hot summers, and for other reasons, it became necessary to expand the operation to larger quarters at Morristown, New Jersey. The school continues there today, and several similar schools are in operation now in various parts of the country. Each school operates independently, but all have similar objectives. (Please see the list of schools at the end of Chapter Eight).

Thanks to the untiring efforts of Morris Frank, Dorothy Eustis and other pioneers, the New Jersey State Legislature eventually passed a law making it illegal to refuse admittance to any visually impaired person accompanied by a guide dog. Other states quickly followed, and today guide dogs are admitted in public places in every state. Most of the schools provide dogs to the visually impaired without cost, or at a minimal cost, operating entirely on donated funds. They receive no federal, state or local tax money. They deserve your support.

Today, 16,000 guide dogs are successfully leading their visually impaired human partners in the United States.

The number is growing by five to seven per cent per year.

Order Form

Ship to: (Please Print)

Name:		
Address:		
City:	State:	Zip:

USA $14.95 ea.	
Canada $17.95 ea.	
Postage & Handling $2.50 Per Book	
FL Residents Add 6% Sales Tax	
Total Amount Enclosed	

Make check or money order payable to:
Marian Lund Modlin
c/o GUNTER
POB 6235
Zephyrhills, FL 33540

Order Form

Ship to: (Please Print)

Name:		
Address:		
City:	State:	Zip:

USA $14.95 ea.	
Canada $17.95 ea.	
Postage & Handling $2.50 Per Book	
FL Residents Add 6% Sales Tax	
Total Amount Enclosed	

Make check or money order payable to:
Marian Lund Modlin
c/o GUNTER
POB 6235
Zephyrhills, FL 33540